THE SLITHERERS

The obscure village of Coxwold had suddenly become the centre of attention of every daily newspaper. People from all over had descended upon it, investigating, questioning, and sending reports to London. Something had happened in a nearby wheat field which had reduced two normal, healthy men to insanity and death. The police, suspecting foul play, lacked any evidence. So what could it be that had driven the victims to madness? This was unlike any crime ever before recorded . . .

JOHN RUSSELL FEARN

THE SLITHERERS

Complete and Unabridged

LINFORD
Leicester

First published in Great Britain

First Linford Edition
published 2009

British Library CIP Data

Fearn, John Russell, *1908 – 1960.*
   The slitherers
   1. Detective and mystery stories.
   2. Large type books.
   I. Title
   823.9'12–dc22

   ISBN 978–1–84782–681–7

Published by
F. A. Thorpe (Publishing)
Anstey, Leicestershire

Set by Words & Graphics Ltd.
Anstey, Leicestershire
Printed and bound in Great Britain by
T. J. International Ltd., Padstow, Cornwall

This book is printed on acid-free paper

1

Queer happenings in Coxwold

I had been looking at the object for a long time and its very strangeness fascinated me. After all it is not common to behold a dome of blue glass — or at least that was what it looked like — perching in the midst of the tranquil English countryside

How I had come upon this object doesn't really signify, but I suppose I ought to lead up to it. Matter of fact, I was on holiday at the time, a camera holiday, and my wanderings had taken me into southern England in the midst of a blazing July. Then, one mid-afternoon, after toiling up a long slope which somehow looked as though it had once been a paved roadway, I came across the blue glass dome.

There it was, right before me, surrounded by the wilderness of the countryside. The bright sun, the soft

1

wind, the twittering of birds — all the adjuncts of the countryside grouped around this monstrous silent thing. As I said, I just stood and stared.

The object was pretty nearly four miles square I reckoned, and some twenty feet in height. But the odd thing was there seemed to be no way of getting into it. For over two hours I prowled round this huge black greenhouse, taking a photograph or two, and all the time wondering how the blazes such a thing came to be here in the lonely countryside. It seemed to be made of glass — the one-way variety, for I could see nothing through it. It just reflected the glare of the midsummer sun in one purply-black dome.

So I passed the afternoon, mystifying myself more deeply with every moment. It was only the need for tea that got me on the move again at last, and I finished up at a local inn that was still within sight — very distinctly — of the dome.

'What is it? That thing?' I asked mine host, as he brought me beer and ham sandwiches onto the inn's little garden.

'You be meanin' the blue dome, sir?' He cocked a curiously grim eye upon me.

'Naturally. I never saw anything quite like it. Is it some sort of building?'

He was silent for a moment, his thumbs latched in the strings of his apron.

'No, it's not a building,' he said finally. 'It's a shield — and y'might call it a sort of monument too. A monument to something mighty queer which happened when I was a lad . . . '

I waited, reflecting that that must have been some time ago. He was well into his sixties I judged.

'You won't be much age, sir, will you?' he asked presently.

'Me? I'm thirty-two.'

'Aye. You wouldn't be born when the Slitherers were here. That dome was used to deal with 'em . . . '

I slowly picked up my glass of beer. 'Slitherers did you say? What the hell are Slitherers?'

'That's the funny part — Ain't anybody knows, really — save perhaps some of these scientific fellers. I did hear it might have bin the end of the world if they hadn't built that blue dome.' He hauled across a chair and sat on it. 'I've got a bit of time to spare so I could tell about it . . . I'm always being asked,' he finished broodingly.

'Be glad if you would,' I told him, and started on my ham sandwiches — but believe me I soon forgot all about them as he told his tale. How much of it was true I cannot say, but I suppose it could be checked by reference to old newspapers. Anyway, see what you think.

In 2010 the mystery of flying saucers reared itself again. The almost forgotten controversies of earlier years received a fresh impetus by the appearance in March of a veritable flock of the strange craft. Most of them were seen to be moving with enormous velocity and trailing a queer grey smoke screen that settled rapidly into a dense mist. In all parts of the world visitations were noted and prompt measures were taken — uselessly. The world's fastest planes and guided missiles carrying movie cameras were powerless to keep up with the disk-shaped objects, and in most cases the mist-screen acted as a complete visual blanket.

Almost before anybody could do anything the saucers had come and gone — leaving behind them a settling pearl-grey mist which, the experts assumed, had been used solely as a smoke screen. That was all. The hue and cry and banner headlines faded out and the visit of the saucers, en masse, was forgotten, except for one or two scientists who made the usual announcement that there was no doubt whatever that Earth was being watched.

Being watched did not, however, interfere with the normal pursuits of Mr. and Mrs. Citizen. Work and pleasure continued as usual and nobody was particularly concerned. There were perhaps one or two *puzzled* people, mostly in the farming community — so puzzled indeed that a conference of farmers was called for in London — whilst in other countries other members of the rural fraternity congregated at the meetings in their particular capitals.

Out of these specially reported meetings there emerged the fact that the value of wheat in particular would have to undergo radical changes for the simple reason that nearly every farmer was growing wheat over nine feet high. It was unbelievable, and yet a fact. Even the most efficient fertilizers and modern methods could hardly account for this gargantuan result, and in the main, farmers did not know whether to be pleased or worried about it. Certainly something would have to be done in regard to the currency value since for every acre of wheat there was now approximately three times the normal yield.

Some suggested naively that it was the unusually hot, fine summer in England that had caused this attack of giantism — but that did not explain why almost every agricultural country had got the same result. Certainly it was peculiar, but as usual it did not interest the average man and woman for long. The curious mystery of gargantuanism faded from the public eye and became the plaything of the professionals.

One professional in particular was assigned the task of trying to solve the problem for the British Ministry of Agriculture — Hartley Norcross by name, an analytical chemist in the Ministry's scientific division. And so Hartley Norcross came to the little village of Coxwold in Hertfordshire, choosing this spot as about the heart of the farming community.

Here Norcross talked with farmers, lived with farmers, and drank with farmers in the local pub.

He wrote lengthy reports back to the Ministry, but in each one he unashamedly confessed that he had not solved the problem. The reply was swift and to the point: Find something or come back to London.

Faced with this ultimatum, Norcross made a last, desperate effort. That same evening he cornered one of the leading farmers in the pub.

'I've got to get to the bottom of this business, Mr. Henshaw,' Norcross was briefly explanatory concerning London's dictum. 'The Ministry is a bit short-tempered about my having got no results. What can you tell me?'

'I don't see there's anything more,' the farmer responded. 'I can only repeat what I've said before. We're all growing wheat the like of which you never saw before. All of us.'

Norcross led the way to a corner table and ordered beer. 'I think I'll try a fresh track, Mr. Henshaw. Is it only wheat which is affected?'

'You've seen my farm and pasture land.'

'I know, but I looked particularly at the wheat. How about other things like — like turnips, carrots, and potatoes?'

'Fairly big yield, I'd say, but nothing like the outsize in wheat.'

'How does the barley behave?'

'Normal.'

'Yes. That's the damnable thing.'

Norcross slitted his eyes and took a drink of his beer. He was a small, officious man with a long, inquiring nose.

'What's so damnable?' the farmer asked, wiping his moustache.

8

'Why, the wheat growing whilst the barley doesn't. One could picture some kind of fertilizer that has an unusually powerful property causing giantism, but it wouldn't single out wheat and leave the barley untouched. That wouldn't make sense.'

'No. But then, nothing does in this business.'

'Would you say,' Norcross persisted, 'that each plant has an individual plan of nourishment? I mean, would a fertilizer for turnips act equally well for — say, rose bushes?'

'It might — and then again it might not. There are rose bushes and rose bushes.'

'The wheat is perfect? It is not deprived of essential ingredients by being outsize?'

Henshaw shook his head. 'Everything's there — full to overflowing. The finest wheat the world has ever known. If you ask me, Mr. Norcross, it's a warning. There'll be a famine after this, and the Good Lord is giving us the chance to fill our storehouses.'

Being a materialist, Norcross took no

notice of spiritual warnings. Instead he did what he ought to have done at first — took a sample of the soil and fertilizer used on Farmer Henshaw's fields and returned with it to the Ministry's Laboratories. Not that this did any particular good, either, for analysis showed the fertilizer to contain all the ingredients one would expect of a good plant food — bar one, which was presumably a secret of the manufacturers.

This one ingredient worried Norcross more than somewhat. When he had completed his analysis he sat at the bench, studying the results of his work.

'Nitrates, phosphates, sodium, they're all here,' he muttered. 'But what the hell's this one?'

'This one' had no name and was brownish grey when detached from its brother elements. It refused to respond to any reagent, and as far as Norcross could tell did not enter into any of the known tables of elements, either. It had something of the quality of brown dung, yet it wasn't that either.

Finally Norcross rose to his feet,

glanced at his watch, and then searched the telephone directory. In another moment he was speaking to the manager of one of the biggest fertilizer concerns in the country.

'This is confidential,' Norcross said briefly. 'The Ministry of Agriculture, Scientific Division, speaking. I'm Norcross. I understand from one Mr. Henshaw that you supply him with all his fertilizer?'

'Quite right,' the manager agreed. 'Can I help you?'

'You can. Give me the formula for your X-1 fertilizer, specially intended for crops.'

There was a brief delay, then the manager complied. The more ingredients he reeled off the more puzzled Norcross looked. At length he said:

'You are quite certain that is the formula you sold to Mr. Henshaw?'

'Why yes. Not only to him, either, but to hundreds of other farmers as well.'

'I see. Thanks very much. Just checking up.'

Norcross put the telephone back on its

rest and stared in front of him. The peculiar thing was that, though the ingredients themselves had been mentioned, the proportions were utterly different from Norcross's analysis — and even more surprising, the brown substance had not been referred to at all.

'Something had been added to the fertilizer since it was sold to Henshaw,' Norcross said, to the empty reaches of the laboratory. Then he shook his head. 'No, not that. The proportions aren't even the same. And there's this brown substance.'

He considered the matter for a moment or two, then went into an even more exhaustive test — this time solely on the brown substance. For close to an hour he studied the stuff through the electronic microscope, comparing its strange makeup with all the known photographs and plates of different fertilizing material, but in none of them could he find even a near match.

'Looks like some sort of animal matter,' Norcross mused. 'That isn't unusual in fertilizer, of course, but if it wasn't put in by the makers, where did it come from?

And how does it happen to be selective in choosing wheat in preference to anything else?'

Quite frankly, Norcross did not know what to make of it, but on the reasonable assumption that he could not be alone in his bafflement he contacted other agriculture headquarters in other countries to see what their version was. And it was the same as his own: The fertilizer contained an unknown quantity, and nobody knew how it had gotten there. Even where the fertilizer had not come from the same manufacturer as Henshaw's, there was still that unaccountable brown ingredient to be accounted for.

And it couldn't be accounted for. Therein lay the problem. Meanwhile, amidst the titanic cornstalks of Coxwold, life was continuing as usual — or rather, existence was. The harvest was so far advanced, and so unnatural, that Farmer Henshaw and his neighbours were already gathering in the results of their labours. A quarter of the cornstalks lay bare, showing promise of a second amazing crop under the sweltering sunshine

— and, in a manner not uncommon, there were holidaymakers assisting in the harvest, and picnicking in their spare time.

Two of the holidaymakers — assistants, the youngest of the whole batch, chose on one particularly hot afternoon to have tea in the shelter of the unreaped cornfield. There was nothing unusual about this since there was ample shelter from the sun amidst the lusty yellow growths. Besides, the youth of the two picnickers — they were neither of them more than eighteen — made them regard the unnatural forest as a centre of attraction.

So they ate and drank and lounged, lying on their backs at the base of the growths, glimpsing the occasional views of the cobalt sky as the wind stirred the fantastic corn above their heads.

A boy and a girl, supremely happy, of the same age, deep in a forest of yellow and enjoying every minute of it. What more natural than this? Grim situations have arisen from far less simple beginnings.

'Harry,' the girl said, thinking. 'Harry,

isn't it a bit queer about this corn? About it being so big, I mean? I never saw anything like it.'

Harry shrugged, tossing the problem from his shoulders with the inconsequence of youth.

'Neither did I, but it's just the place to hide out in. It's hot working in the field. Least, I think so.'

There was silence for a moment between them.

Rita drained a mineral water bottle and then flung it to one side. It vanished immediately amidst the growths, and Harry looked at her grimly.

'That's going to be a nice thing for a reaper to find in its track,' he said. 'Go and pick it up. What's the use of all these signs about keeping the countryside tidy?'

Rita sighed and scrambled to her feet, clutching to her a half-wrapped parcel of meat-paste sandwiches. Muttering to herself she went through the yellow undergrowth in search of the mineral bottle, and Harry watched her go. He could not help noticing the amazing height of the cornstalks in comparison to her own five feet. The stalks themselves were as thick as bamboo poles, and pretty nearly as hard.

After a while Rita returned, the empty bottle in one hand and sandwiches fiercely clutched in the other.

'You and your bottle!' she protested. 'I've lost half my sandwiches in getting it back.'

She put it down beside her as she squatted, and Harry looked at her in surprise.

'Lost half your sandwiches? How do you mean?'

'They fell out of the parcel, that's what I mean!'

'Well, couldn't you have picked them up?'

'What? Covered in dirty old fertilizer? You know how it sticks to meat paste! Hardly!'

'Ummm,' Harry said, and let the subject drop. Though disinclined to argue, he had to admit the logic of Rita's observation. Meat paste and fertilizer would hardly mix. And Rita said no more, save to complain about the scarcity of sandwiches. She did not know any more than Harry that she had participated in a world-shaking event.

After their somewhat abbreviated tea they resumed the labours of gathering corn, and they did the same next day, and the day after that as the weather still continued blazingly fine. Each day they sought the slowly diminishing region of the cornfield for their tea-break, with Rita taking extra care of her sandwiches and mineral bottle disposal.

'I wonder,' Harry mused, 'how much longer this kind of weather is going to continue? It's been at it for about eight weeks already with hardly a cloud, and there isn't a sign of a break even yet. Pity the holiday's up tomorrow. I don't feel at all like going back to city life.'

'No more than I do. If we had plenty of money we could do a lot of things . . . ' Rita lay back, hands behind her head, and surveyed the patchwork of sunny blue sky overhead. 'Harry, why is it always such a struggle to get hold of money?'

Harry did not reply. He was staring fixedly into the depths of the cornstalks.

Presently he shut his eyes and then opened them again.

'Probably the heat,' he said at length, and Rita turned lazily to look at him.

'Why does the heat make it difficult to get hold of money? That doesn't make sense.'

'What I'm looking at doesn't make sense either. That's why I said it must be the heat.'

There was an odd note in Harry's voice that brought Rita from her reclining position to sudden alertness. She followed the direction of Harry's gaze into the bamboo-like jungle, and for a while failed completely to detect what had fascinated him. Then she saw it — or rather them. Reddish-grey objects like tadpoles darting up, down, and around the cornstalks with such prodigious velocity they were a mere blur. Sometimes there seemed to be only a couple of them, then at others a good dozen. It was difficult to tell.

'What are they?' Rita questioned, surprised.

'Dunno. Sort of dragonflies . . . '

Dragonflies without wings? Things that

didn't even look like dragonflies? Things that travelled with terrific speed, darting about with the speed of minnows? Harry realized how utterly wrong he was even as he spoke.

'How many are there?' Some instinct of precaution set Rita rising slowly to her feet.

'No idea. 'Bout a dozen actually, I'd say. Looks like more because they move so fast they're almost in two places at once.'

Rita looked for a little while and then shuddered. In spite of herself she felt an instinctive revulsion, without really knowing why she felt it.

'They're — they're *horrible!*' she exclaimed suddenly. 'Look at the way they just — just slither round and over everything.'

'So they do!' Harry had not noticed it before, but now that Rita came to mention it he saw what she meant. The things were definitely serpentine in their movements, yet faster than any reptile ever created.

Suddenly Harry realized that he did

not know what they were. He was fairly knowledgeable on matters of nature and so forth, but never in his life had he seen anything like these things before.

'I'm going to take a closer look,' he said finally, and with sudden resolution strode forward. Rita half made to follow him, then that curious instinct warned her to stay put.

No such instincts troubled the materialistic Harry. He went close to the blur of grey objects and watched them intently. In the brief seconds of the creatures' repose he could see a tiny, froglike face with beady eyes and tightly clamped mouth. The things didn't look harmful. The pity was that they couldn't be classified.

'Queer,' Harry muttered to himself, and turned to go — but that was as far as he got. As though shot from a gun three or four of the creatures literally flung themselves at him like tiny projectiles — and stuck. With the tenacity of leeches they clung to his forehead and temples, resisting all his efforts to brush them off.

The instant Rita saw what had

happened she stood for a moment in sheer horror, staring at the objects depending from Harry's forehead — then swung round and fled through the cornstalks to the freedom of the sunshine and fresh air. There she slowed up, waiting with mixed feelings for Harry to appear. Here she felt safer. There was room to turn around. In the distance the rest of the holidaymakers-cum-harvesters were having their tea. If the situation proved too much for her she could always call on them for assistance.

Moments passed. Rita waited, unable to analyse what she was thinking. Then after a while Harry came stumbling into view, groping his way with the uncertainty of a blind man. The slithering objects were no longer anchored to his forehead, but there were blood streaks where they had been. Rita took a step backwards, immensely uncertain.

Harry looked at her, but for some reason he did not speak. He still had the blind man's way of walking, feeling his way in front of him as though there were a barrier. And with every step nearer which he took Rita became convinced of something horrible.

This was not Harry. It couldn't be. The drooling lips, the mindless stare of his eyes, the uncertain movements. He looked like an idiot, in every sense of the word.

Suddenly he fell, and stayed fallen. He was not unconscious; just incapable of moving forward or standing upright. Rita began to run, towards the holidaymakers with their tea, then in the midst of it she suddenly didn't know anything any more.

The sun was well down when Rita became conscious again. By degrees she assimilated the fact that she was lying on a couch in Farmer Henshaw's parlour. He himself was at a table, stern and worried. Across the room, gazing out into the sunset, stood his wife. These were the immediate registrations in Rita's mind as she slowly stirred.

Her movement instantly brought Henshaw across to her. The troubled lines of his weather-beaten face relaxed somewhat.

'Better, Miss Haslam?' he inquired.

'Yes, much better.' Rita frowned to herself. 'I fainted, or something, didn't I?'

'Yes — you fainted. In fact you've been unconscious quite a long time.' Mrs. Henshaw drifted over to her husband's side and stood looking intently at Rita.

'I'm all right now,' Rita said, with more conviction than she felt. 'How's Harry? Is he all right now?'

'Harry,' the farmer said quietly, 'is dead.'

Rita stared incredulously. 'Dead? But he can't be! There was nothing that could kill him.'

Farmer and wife looked at one another. Then Henshaw cleared his throat and avoided meeting Rita's eyes as he spoke.

'We picked up Harry just after you fainted. He couldn't speak. There was a look in his eyes that was . . . well, just nothing; the sort of look you'd expect to see from a person who has no mind. The look of an imbecile. He couldn't even walk! We had to lift him up, and they took him to hospital. I heard an hour ago that he was dead. I've just come back from breaking the news to his people.'

23

Rita said nothing. With a bemused stare she looked straight in front of her.

'The boy couldn't suddenly have lost his reason like that!' Mrs. Henshaw declared. 'It doesn't make sense. He hadn't even any leanings that way. A strong, cheerful, happy young man if ever there was one — and then suddenly!'

Silence. There was a queer conviction of foreboding, of nameless evil lurking somewhere in the cornstalks; perhaps —

'The — the slitherers!' Rita exclaimed suddenly, jumping up and swinging giddily. 'The slitherers must have done it!'

'The what?' Henshaw asked sharply.

'I don't suppose that makes sense,' Rita hurried on, 'but that is what I'd call them. Tadpoles that move with lightning speed and cling to the flesh like leeches. I remember Harry had some sticking to his head and face.'

'Come now, child . . . ' Mrs. Henshaw's arm went gently round Rita's shoulders. 'What are you saying? Is this something you dreamed about that you're telling us?'

'Of course it isn't!' Rita's voice was

sharp with near hysteria. 'They were out there in the cornfield where Harry and I had our tea . . . ' and she went on swiftly to relate the whole incident. When she had finished the farmer and his wife looked at each other again.

'I'll look into this!' Henshaw declared abruptly, striding to the door. 'If there are things like that in my cornfield they won't be there long, I promise you. Look after the child, Edie,'

Then he was gone. Rita, quivering, sat down on the sofa, burying her face in her hands. She could not analyse her emotions. She was still suffering from both reaction and grief. Not that she had consciously been in love with Harry, but she had certainly known him well, and the knowledge of how strangely and horribly he had met his death had come as a blinding shock.

'I'm sure it was the slitherers!' she kept insisting, and Mrs. Henshaw sat down slowly beside her.

'Easy, child, easy. If there is anything there my husband will find it, never fear.'

Rita jerked up her head, gripped with a

sudden premonition.

'He shouldn't have gone, Mrs. Henshaw! Your husband should not have gone! It's dangerous. I'm sure of it!'

Mrs. Henshaw smiled. 'Don't worry, love. My hubby knows what he's doing.'

With an effort Rita forced herself to be calm

'There'll be an inquest about Harry Cotterill,' Mrs. Henshaw resumed. 'You'll have to say what happened in the cornfield; but please take it easy and don't let your fancy run away with you. I'll have a word with your parents before the inquest and maybe they can — '

Mrs. Henshaw broke off and Rita sat in frozen silence, for suddenly out of the evening there had come a scream — the ghastly, insufferable scream of a strong man overwhelmed. It quivered down into silence and outwardly nothing was changed

But Rita knew — and so did Mrs. Henshaw. The Slitherers!

The following morning the newspapers had something to feast upon — something apart from atomic bombs, celebrity scandal, and political slanging. Practically every daily concentrated a searchlight on the queer happenings in Coxwold. Overnight, the obscure English village became a sensation-spot. It seemed that everybody under the sun came to Coxwold during the night, asking questions, writing reports, wanting to know this and that, and telephoning it back to London.

Something in the wheat field had reduced two perfectly healthy men of differing ages to mindless imbecility and death. But what had reduced them?

Rita told her story of the Slitherers — a popular name which caught on with the public — and so of course there were investigations into the two acres of corn remaining in the field. And nothing happened. Not a tadpole in sight. Just the corn and nothing else. The first shades of doubt began to appear, and those whose duty it was to discuss the matter hardly knew where to start.

The police in particular were suspicious. They suspected there had been foul play somewhere, but without any evidence of it their hands were tied. Further, what could it be that had reduced the victims to imbecility? This was unlike any crime ever before recorded. In the absence of anything else, death by misadventure had to be returned

The Ministry of Agriculture executives were frankly astounded. Not for one moment did they credit the story of slithering tadpoles, though they were prepared to admit that perhaps there was something peculiar about that particular cornfield. After all, the corn was phenomenal, so probably anything could happen. Hartley Norcross was assigned once again to dig up anything he could find, particularly as the people of Coxwold had fled their dwellings as a precautionary measure.

So the long-nosed Norcross returned to Coxwold, to find it literally the deserted village. Every house was bolted and barred, every farm and store was shut tight. Not a soul moved in the hot summer afternoon. Even cattle had been taken away, and the only living things were birds and insects.

'Nice hell of a job to send a man on,' Norcross commented, strolling down the village high street. 'Who do they think I am, anyway? Sherlock Holmes?'

By no stretch of imagination could Norcross have been bracketed with the famous fictional investigator — but he had nonetheless a very inquisitive turn of mind, as was plainly evidenced by his abnormally long nose. He had arrived in Coxwold to find something out — and this meant doing it if it killed him.

But, like those who had searched before him, Norcross failed to discover anything. The village itself was normal, even if deserted — and the stripped cornfields had nothing unusual to offer. Norcross found himself wandering through the fields in the blaze of the summer sun, all kinds of theories turning over in his mind.

It was at this point that he came upon the crumbled remains of meat paste sandwiches, the remains of the tea Rita had dropped some days before in her search for an abandoned mineral water bottle.

Norcross stood looking down at the remains, his brows knitted. By now most of the bread was curled up like old boot soles, and much of it had been pecked away by the ever-avid birds. But there were still brown smears of meat paste, fluffy with mould in parts. Norcross did not know why, but something about those ancient bits of bread and meat paste interested him, particularly so where brown plant fertilizer had mixed with the meat paste and produced a golden-brown amalgam, which gleamed stickily in the torrid sunshine.

Norcross was remembering the fertilizer samples that he had personally analysed, and particularly the unknown brown substance. Suppose — ? He squinted into the sunshine on the edge of a thought. Well, just suppose . . .

Presently Norcross went down on his knees and prodded the sticky, syrupy substance with the end of a pencil. To his infinite horror the sticky substance — which he presumed was a mixture of meat paste and fertilizer — stirred and jumped visibly, as though it had a life of its own.

Quickly Norcross withdrew his pencil and reflected. Perhaps he had been out in the sun too long. No, it wasn't that either, for even as he watched the gummy mess retracted itself and then went through a mysterious gyration. Before his very eyes he saw something forming — a small, eel-like body, a blunted head, two tightly shut eyes. It was no delusion. It was some form of life having its birth in the syrupy cocoon that shimmered in the heat.

The guardian angel that watches over little children and drunks also whispered something in Norcross's ear at that moment. He jammed his pencil in his pocket and retreated backwards along the needlepoints of the cornstalks. When he had reached what he considered was a safe distance he crouched to watch.

Nor did he need to watch for long. The thing he had seen forming abruptly rose from the sticky mess that had been its birthplace. It shot to a distance of perhaps twenty feet and there came to a dead stop in midair and hovered. Without wings, without anything. It looked exactly like a slug with the head of a snake. In size it was not particularly big, but it certainly radiated a curious suggestion of evil. It

31

was repulsive, horribly alien to a stripped cornfield and a quiet summer afternoon.

Norcross licked his lips and remained motionless, waiting. At the back of his mind was the thought that the girl Rita Haslam had not been exaggerating. The things *did* exist, but this one — at the moment anyway — did not seem to have done anything to justify the appellation of 'Slitherer.'

But that was where Norcross guessed wrong. He had just come to this point in his mental debate when the object suddenly moved again — straight for him. It came with the velocity of a bullet dead to its target. Norcross had only a split second. The thing seemed to be hurtling for his head so he threw up a hand to protect himself. With a resounding *'Thwack!'* the object struck his hand — the back thereof — and stuck relentlessly, held by some kind of suction that was mercilessly solid and tight.

Sweating, Norcross shook his hand fiercely, but the hideous-looking thing refused to budge. So Norcross tore at it with his other hand, and still failed to drag it free. At the same time he was conscious of a tingling sensation, rather like that generated by a jellyfish.

'Damn you, get off!' Norcross breathed, and slammed his hand down on the sharp barbs left by the cornstalks. Jolted with what must have been intolerable pain, the weird object bit savagely, tearing a piece out of the back of Norcross's hand. He gazed at it stupidly, wondering just what was happening in this deserted cornfield.

Then fury and panic got the better of him. From a distance he must have cut a ludicrous figure as he fought with himself, slapping his bleeding hand against himself, or again crashing it down on the cornstalk barbs.

Until at last he got results. Weakened by the onslaught the thing suddenly gave up the struggle and detached itself, hurtling several feet into the air, then streaking away towards some unknown destination.

Norcross watched it go, his legs shaking. Then he pulled out his handkerchief and wrapped it round his bleeding hand, whilst he wondered if maybe there had been venom in those deadly jaws.

2

Evolution

The first living thing the isolated Slitherer came across was Sheila Danebury, a little girl of six, on her way from her father's farm to the village of Great Prexton, neighbour village to the ill-starred Coxwold. Little Sheila was entirely content with life as she tripped along, a bunch of wild flowers in her hand, the hot sunlight glancing through her fair hair.

When the Slitherer forced itself on her vision, she just stopped and stared at it. It was on top of a roadside hedge, its sides heaving with the effort of breathing. Actually of course it was in a good deal of pain from the savage beating it had received against the cornstalk barbs.

Then Sheila moved, her childish curiosity stirred. The Slitherer watched her advance from its beady eyes — then came that peculiar, bullet-like forward movement. It shot from the hedge top to Sheila's forehead in a matter of seconds. She crashed instantly into the dust of the lane and struggled for a moment or two to drag the hideous thing from her head. Then gradually she relaxed and finally became limp . . . The Slitherer remained on her forehead for a moment or two and then shot skywards, leaving behind a crumpled figure in a dusty cotton frock, her posy of flowers wilting in the sunlight . . .

She was lying thus when Norcross found her. From the cornfield he had followed the natural path that took him to the lane, and automatically he had come to Sheila. Instantly he ran forward, feeling quickly for her heart and at the same time looking at the reddish bruise on her forehead . . . As he had expected, there was no life remaining.

'The filthy killer!' Norcross whispered, looking first at the dead child, then at his own still bleeding hand. 'The filthy, dirty killer . . .'

If Norcross had had any doubts before about pursuing this business to its conclusion, he certainly had them no longer. The dead child in the lane was enough for him. He'd solve this mystery if it took him the rest of his life . . . But for the moment, he had to attend to more practical things.

Having no idea where the girl had come from he lifted her body in his arms and began carrying her to whatever happened to be the first habitation he came across — which was the farm from which she had come. In dazed silence farmer Danebury and his wife watched as Sheila was laid on the parlour sofa; then the farmer's sharp eyes began to aim questions.

'For the love of God, what happened?' he demanded hoarsely. 'Who — who attacked our Sheila?'

'A Slitherer,' Norcross said briefly. 'Heard of 'em?'

'Aye,' the wife confirmed, looking up from beside Sheila's body. 'The things that emptied yonder Coxwold.'

'Right . . . ' Norcross wagged his bleeding hand. 'And they're still there, or at least one of them was. I'll gamble it

36

was the one which killed your daughter after it had attacked me . . . Got some water? I'd like to wash my hand.'

Only half aware of what he was doing the farmer led the way into a flagged kitchen and Norcross went to work with the pump. Apparently his hand was not poisoned, but it hurt like the devil, particularly on the back where the horror had fastened itself.

'Who are you, mister?' the farmer asked grimly, after a moment or two.

'Hartley Norcross, analytical chemist of the Ministry of Agriculture. I've been sent down to investigate Coxwold.'

'How did you come across my Sheila, Mister Norcross?'

Norcross aimed a sharp look. 'Don't get off on the wrong track, my friend. I came across the child automatically.'

'So you say. I'd like a bit of proof of it — '

Norcross hesitated; then, 'I can understand how you feel. You'd best call a doctor and have him take a look at your youngster.'

'What for? She's dead, ain't she? The

doctor can't do anything.'

'Unfortunately no, but at least he can give some opinion as to the cause of death.'

The farmer hesitated. It was obvious he was thinking a good deal — but something in Norcross's expression made him refrain from further comment. Norcross was no murderer, no child sadist. There was about him an air of purpose — and then again there was on his hand the same curious imprint as on Sheila's forehead. The same thing that had attacked her had also attacked him.

'I've things to do,' Norcross said briefly. 'I'm going back to the cornfield to see if there are any more of these infernal things. There might be: I had the doubtful joy of seeing this particular one hatch.'

'And we're just left with our little girl dead?' the farmer asked slowly.

'I sympathise with you in all con-science, but can't you see that this business has got to be rooted out before others are killed? There's decidedly deadly business afoot. Here!' Norcross raked out his wallet and handed over a card. 'That's where you and the Police can get in touch with me . . . '

And Norcross wasted no more time. He left the farm full of grim purpose and retraced his way to the cornfield. When he gained it he approached warily towards the sticky mess he had originally seen — and then he stood looking at something that seemed pretty close to the impossible. There were more Slitherers in the very process of being formed. Norcross counted half a dozen of them — small tadpole objects as yet, but definitely full of life.

For a moment or two he stood considering, faced with a problem that had no parallel in his experience. He had no weapons, no acid, no anything with which to destroy these things — whatever they were. The only thing he had got was a cigarette lighter, and an idea.

Norcross retreated to a short distance, gathered a few dried twigs, and then lighted them. There was a puff of smoke on the windless air and then as he had expected, the corn stubs took the flame to themselves and began to spread a crackling, burning area around the mess where the mysterious things were evolving . . .

His eyes smarting with smoke Norcross watched the blackening, blazing expanse. He knew quite well that the cornfield would soon be entirely in flames — indeed that the fire might spread further — but he considered he was justified. That is until out of the smoke six full grown Slitherers came shooting with projectile-like swiftness.

Norcross saw them just in time and flung himself flat. The six of them shot clean over his head, and to his infinite relief they showed no signs of turning back. Evidently they were wary of fire and had no intention of braving it.

Norcross got to his feet again and plunged through the choking smoke to the sticky area. It was still there, looking the same as before. The flames had not reached it but had formed a black area around it.

'Analysis,' Norcross muttered. 'The only thing . . . Those six brutes which escaped must have been evolved enough to look after themselves.'

Making up his mind he started at a run for his car. The course took him down the lane where Sheila Danebury had died, past her parents' farm, and to the deserted main road where the car was still standing. It only took a moment for Norcross to dig out a tyre lever and an empty can with a big mouth that he normally used for oil. Armed with these he went back to the merrily burning cornfield and spent some time collecting as much of the syrupy mess as he could manage. Then, satisfied that the fire was dying as it reached the limits of the stripped field, he returned to his car with his sample tin held cautiously in front of him. He put it in the boot, slammed down the lid, and hoped for the best. There lurked at the back of his mind the fear that something might hatch even as he drove back to London, but that was one of the things he would have to chance.

Meanwhile six known Slitherers — no, seven, if one included the injured one which had attacked and killed Sheila — had vanished into the outer world from the cornfield — and there might even be others, many others, that had propagated in the time before Norcross had come on the scene.

Where were they? What would they do next?

And most important of all, what the devil did they want anyhow?

These were the questions that preoccupied the long-nosed Norcross as he drove along the sweltering, dusty roads back to the city. Of course, there was only one answer — blast the cornfield with flamethrowers, bombs, or something. That might kill the source of it, yes, but what about those things that had got away?

And while Norcross drove other things were happening. There was the case of the family on picnic two counties away from the scene of his own experience.

For some five minutes the lazy picnickers — father, mother, young son and daughter — had been watching the curious gyrations of something in a nearby tree. The thing moved so fast they could hardly follow its movement with the eye.

'I'm not much up in the country life,'

father said, yawning. 'Looks to me like some kind of slug. Yet on the other hand I'd say it is more like a serpent . . . '

'Serpent!' his wife echoed in horror.

They didn't exchange any more conversation.

With the usual terrific velocity common to the Slitherers this particular one shot into action. The father went down first, and though they were scared to death mother, son, and daughter did what they could to rip away the frightful leechlike thing as it clung to father's forehead. Even so they were beaten. The Slitherer moved only when it was ready, and then it was to the wife, and lastly to the whimpering children.

In half an hour four dazed, mindless human beings stumbled in the midst of the picnic they had been enjoying so happily — and in another half hour every one of them was dead. Satiated, back in the tree whence it had come in the first place, the Slitherer surveyed the green world, its merciless jaws tightly shut, its unblinking reptilian eyes watching, watching.

Another case, completely remote from the picnickers, involved the haymakers of Tilton Menbury, another remote southern hamlet. Six of them went down after a furious fight, leaving dazed farm labourers, drawn by the sound of the struggle, to figure out what had happened. And this time the Slitherer concerned did not stay around the district but hurtled northwards, bent on some mission of its own.

In the space of one short summer afternoon several lives had been sacrificed to the Slitherers, and the man who had sworn to find the answer arrived at the Ministry of Agriculture laboratories towards tea-time, fifteen minutes indeed before they closed for the night.

Norcross heaved a sigh of relief as he took his sample tin from the boot. Apparently there had not been any further propagation. Carefully he transported it through the main lab to the particular one in which he worked. Adams, one of his co-workers, watched the performance with interest.

'Why such care with a tin of car

grease?' he asked dryly.

'Car grease?' Norcross laughed shortly and tugged off his jacket. 'I only wish it were. It's some kind of amalgam from the Coxwold cornfield, and I'll probably be here for the rest of the night. Might even come into your province, too, if biology is all I think it is.'

Interested, Adams came across the laboratory and peered at the gummy mess in the tin. Then he wrinkled his nose.

'Hell! Certainly stinks, doesn't it?'

Norcross nodded absently. 'I didn't notice it out in the open. Anyway, you know the powers-that-be sent me down to investigate Coxwold and try and find out what had killed a farmer and one of his helpers . . . ? Well, I found out, and nearly got myself wiped out doing it.'

Norcross extended his still damaged and crudely bandaged hand and told the full story.

Adams listened, interested even while he struggled with incredulity.

'I've heard about these tadpole things, of course, from the newspapers, but I thought it was all a lot of rubbish. It seems, from your own experience, that it isn't. But what are they? Where have they come from?'

'No idea.' Norcross tightened his lips. 'But I'm going to find out. I've still got the memory of little Sheila lying there in the lane with her posy of flowers beside her. Killed! Killed just to satisfy the bloodlust of these abominable things. I'm going to find out all about them and then take the greatest pleasure in destroying them.'

'I'd like to work with you,' Adams said. 'Two heads are better than one, anyhow, and if there's anything biological it's in my field. But first, come and have tea with me.'

'Tea? Hell, no! I'm going to get busy.'

'With no refreshment inside you? After all you've been through? Don't be an idiot. Fifteen minutes in the canteen will make all the difference.'

Norcross hesitated, surveyed the sample tin in the sunlight pouring through the window — then he reached for his jacket.

'Okay — maybe you're right at that.'

The two men stayed longer over their

tea and salad than they had intended, but perhaps they had reason. Norcross went again over the details of his activities to date, glad indeed to pour out the facts to somebody who could at least make an attempt to understand them. Norcross knew he had stumbled onto something both big and dangerous, and for that very reason he needed support.

'And here,' came the voice from an unobtrusive loudspeaker which had been dispensing soft music, 'is the first news. There are reports today of extraordinary happenings in various parts of Great Britain, particularly in the area of Coxwold which will be remembered as headlining the news a day or two ago with a report of mysterious tadpole objects. It appears that these tadpole objects have been making their presence felt again. An eight-year-old girl, a picnic party, several haymakers, a solitary commercial traveller, and two girl cyclists, have all fallen victim to these mysterious slayers. Scotland Yard has now taken the matter in hand, and we understand that an official of the Ministry of Agriculture is also investigating. We shall have further details shortly, but until we do everybody is advised to keep a close watch on their safety — particularly in the open country — and should any object be seen which resembles a serpent, and which is usually in the region of a hedge or tree, take every precaution to give it a wide berth, or better still report it to the nearest police station. Now here is an item of political interest . . . '

'Worse than I thought,' Norcross said, as Adams gave him a grim look. 'Those things are striking far and wide . . . I suppose I've Farmer Danebury to thank for handing on my name. I gave him a card.'

'And the sooner you do something to justify your existence, the better,' Adams commented. 'Come on — time we got back to the lab.'

They left immediately and within a few minutes had returned to their laboratory. Norcross did not know why it was, but the moment he crossed the threshold he scented danger. He came to a stop, Adams immediately behind him, looking around.

48

On the face of it everything appeared normal enough — for a moment. Then Norcross reached behind him and gripped Adams' arm tightly. The chemist made a gulping sound in his throat and stared transfixed. There was a Slitherer, half coiled round the top of a huge acid carboy. Its inhuman eyes were fixed unwaveringly on the two men.

'Back out,' Norcross whispered. 'Carefully! I'm used to these damned things . . . '

Adams moved backwards immediately, and attracted by the movement the Slitherer sprang.

It slipped round the top of the carboy like a glittering silver ribbon in the sunlight; then with its incredible velocity it flew straight for Norcross. With only a fraction of time to spare he leapt back into the passage, dragging the door. The impact of the Slitherer as it struck the door shut it, and a crack appeared down one of the top panels. Then there was silence for a moment.

'What happens now?' Adams panted, sweating.

'Nothing.' Norcross's voice was tense.

'Give it a chance to calm down — '

He broke off at the sound of splintering glass.

Gradually the sound died into silence and nothing more seemed to happen.

'I think it's escaped,' Norcross said.

He opened the door again gingerly, and very carefully looked into the laboratory. All was quiet.

One of the windows was shattered, and there was no sign of a Slitherer anywhere.

'Okay,' Norcross muttered. 'It's gone through the window.'

They moved into the laboratory together and Adams scratched his head.

'Maybe I'm dumb, but where did it come from in the first place?'

'The tin.' Norcross nodded to it in the sunshine, exactly where he had left it.

'But there was only jelly, or paste, or something inside the tin when we went to tea.'

'I know. The thing must have been in the midst of the stuff in a state of formation, and while we had tea it evolved.'

'That quickly! Come off it, man!'

'These things,' Norcross said deliberately, 'evolve at a terrific pace, as I've good reason to know. Right now there may be others in the process of evolving — and come to that there are perhaps hundreds more in the Coxwold cornfield. I didn't get all of the jelly by any means; only a scraping.'

'That's a happy thought . . . Well, what's next?'

Norcross moved to the sample tin, lifted it out of the sunshine, and put it down on the central bench. In its depths, amidst the jelly and 'syrup,' were dozens of microscopic specks, rather like carelessly flung cigarette ash. As the two men stared fixedly they could have sworn that the specks were pulsating.

'Future Slitherers — dozens of them,' Norcross said grimly. 'I'd destroy the lot here and now if it wasn't essential to study them.'

Adams pondered. 'What are they? I never saw anything like them before.'

'Neither did anybody else, I fancy. I'd say they're not a product of this world at all, only I can't see how they ever came from another planet . . . There seems to be some connection between plant fertilizer and meat paste sandwiches, though where the devil that fits in I don't know yet.'

Gradually, Adams was getting a firmer grip of the situation. His first fears had given up to an almost fierce desire to investigate the whole business.

'How long before these things evolve?' he asked thoughtfully. 'You say evolution is rapid.'

'True, but . . . ' Norcross thought for a moment. 'It just occurs to me that these things seem to evolve rapidly when there is sunlight. For instance, when the tin was in the car boot and shut off from the sun nothing happened. But when we left the tin in the sun while we had tea a Slitherer, evidently the most advanced of the lot, evolved. We might try putting the tin in the cooler and reducing it almost to freezing point.'

'Good idea.'

Norcross followed up his idea then sat down to think. So far he seemed to have been dodging for safety and witnessing horror. Now the time had come for cold, analytical thinking.

'About these things I know practically nothing,' he said, as Adams waited for observations. 'Leaving the Slitherers themselves for a moment let's concentrate on the stuff that seems to give them birth. First there is fertilizer used in the corn crop — '

'Normal enough. Can't infer anything from that.'

'Don't be too sure! The fertilizer contains an unknown ingredient, which in my own analysis I couldn't fit into anything we know. The manufacturers didn't know what the ingredient was, either. It has been responsible, I think, for a fantastic crop of wheat.'

'All right. Excluding the mystery of the business, we have an unknown ingredient in the fertilizer. Then what have we?'

'Meat paste,' Norcross said. 'And crazy though it is I think the answer lies in that. My idea is to analyze it down to rock bottom and see what we get.'

'Why do that? Contact the manufacturers and ask for the formula.'

Norcross sighed. 'There are hundreds of manufacturers of meat paste, and we don't know which sort this was. It appears that a girl harvester, Rita Haslam by name, originally had the meat paste. Maybe she could remember . . . Hmm, that would take time. No; I'll do my own analysis.'

On this Norcross was determined. He waited until the jelly in the tin was at a temperature just above freezing — which incidentally seemed to have slowed up but not stopped the mysterious life — and then he took the tin from the fridge. Adams watched him scrape some of the jelly onto a microscopic slide and then began operations.

Altogether it took an hour, and the job was done out of line with direct sunlight. Norcross pondered the scratch pad on which he had written his analysis. Adams, in the meantime, blocked the broken window with a big sheet of cardboard.

'Can't separate one from the other,' Norcross said. 'Meat paste from fertilizer, I mean. That leaves us with a good deal of the original fertilizer formula — including the mysterious brown substance which we'll label 'x' — and as far as the meat paste goes it is a standard formula with a fifteen per cent inclusion of dextrone.'

'Dextrone? Seem to have heard of that stuff somewhere.'

'Very probably. It's one of the new vitamin discoveries, included in many canned foods these days. Builds stamina, strong bones, horse teeth, and all the rest of it. At least the public thinks it does ... ' Norcross beat gently with his pencil. 'Which brings us to the interesting speculation of what happens when Dextrone is mixed with this unknown brown element ... Might try it.'

Thereupon began the exacting process of segregating the two elements and then mating them. When it was done Norcross and Adams watched the result — which proved to be merely a sticky brown mess that didn't mean anything.

'Guess again,' Norcross sighed.

'Wait a minute!' Adams said, and pulled the cardboard from the repaired window. 'Try sunlight undiluted. Maybe it's the answer.'

Though he hadn't much faith in the prospect, Norcross nevertheless followed the suggestion, and stood looking at the minute quantity of stuff attentively. Then he frowned. Part of the stuff was very slowly streaking with a wisp of grey. In a matter of seconds it had broken up into specks — once again exactly like cigarette ash.

'Life cells of some sort,' Adams said tensely. 'Very low form of life, too — at least to begin with.'

With the passage of the moments the jelly substance, becoming hotter, turned grey all over, and as before the grey split up into individual units. In the end there were hundreds of minute cells, all living and pulsating, and growing larger.

'Slitherers in the making,' Norcross said grimly. 'Not if I know it.'

He quickly moved the substance out of the sunshine and then threw it into a waste bin. A half bottle of acid followed, and that was that. A filthy stench rose on the air, bubbles and smoke belched out of the waste bin, but in the finish there was nothing left. The stuff had vanished.

'At least we know how to kill it,' Adams said, uncertainly.

'Uh-huh — in the early stages anyway. It's a tougher job when a Slitherer is full-grown . . . Now, let's see where we are.' Norcross looked at his notes and reflected. 'In the light of our present knowledge there is a mysterious element in the plant fertilizer, which causes crops to become gargantuan — but it only happened in the case of wheat, and nothing else. Right! Next, a girl drops sandwiches of meat paste, and the fertilizer and meat paste mixed themselves together in the hot sunlight and produced a gooey mess, out of which come the Slitherers. They're born in the stuff and very rapidly evolve to full size. When they're full grown they are deadly, merciless killers, and they produce imbecility and death.'

Adams said: 'Yes . . . that's it, and it's getting something too big for us to tinker with, Norcross. We need trained scientists — '

'Why?' Norcross asked. 'I'm a trained scientist myself, only agriculture happens to be my line. The basis of this is agricultural. As for the queer biological part, it's all yours. I've a feeling we might solve this between us. We've got part of the way, but we won't really know what we're doing until we find out where the brown element in the fertilizer came from. *That's* the key. After that we have to figure out what these Slitherers are getting at.'

'Nothing, surely? Aren't they just motivated by the blind lust to kill?'

'On the face of it, yes, but usually the victims survive for quite a time after being attacked — adult victims anyway — and the result produced is one of imbecility. As though the mind and reason had been completely blasted.'

'Shock,' Adams said, but Norcross shook his head.

'I'm not so sure. I could imagine it in the case of a child — like young Sheila Danebury for instance — but adults are too tough to succumb so easily. I'm thinking of the way these infernal things fly straight for the forehead. It happened even in my case, but my hand got in the way just in time. Forehead — imbecility — and then death.'

Norcross became silent, following a line of thought. When it led nowhere he gave a shrug.

'How do we start finding out about this unknown ingredient in the fertilizer?' Adams asked. 'Contact the manufacturers again?'

'Wouldn't do any good. They're no wiser than we are. There's perhaps another way. Have a talk with their own chemists and then break down the fertilizer before it leaves the factory and see what it contains? They might be able to name the stuff. Better make that the first move tomorrow.'

'Tonight,' Norcross said, 'I'm going home and study up on all the books I've got concerning chemicals, fertilizers, and what-have-you, then maybe tomorrow I'll be in a better position to tackle the business . . . As for that tin of stuff we'll freeze it overnight. That ought to make it safe enough.'

Carefully he put the tin in the refrigerator and closed the door. Then

Adams asked a question

'Cellular life of this description will divide by fission in order to propagate themselves. Had you thought of that?'

Norcross gave a slight start. 'Frankly, I hadn't. That's more in the biological field. Fission? You mean divide themselves into two?'

'Uh-huh. About the most lowly method of propagation there is, but if that is the principle in the small embryo — and judging from that tin of jelly it certainly is — then the same principle will apply when the things reach maturity.'

Norcross didn't answer. He was just beginning to realise the immensity of the thing he and Adams were trying to fight single-handed. Propagation by fission meant infinite numbers. From the original seven that he knew of, fourteen could appear. From the fourteen, twenty-eight — and from the twenty-eight, fifty-six. And so it could go on — indefinitely, anywhere and anytime. Until at length, unless something desperate were done there would arise a situation similar to that of the millions of eggs of the sea urchin if by some mischance all of them happened to hatch. The Earth would be infested with them.

Slithering, slippery, lightning objects. Killers. And at the moment nobody was realising what was happening — nobody except Norcross and Adams, and they were frankly appalled.

3

Brain Leeches

The wheat field of Coxwold was not dead, even as Norcross had suspected. Long after he had departed, darting grey shapes had taken to the air from amidst the syrupy scum left in the sunshine. It was a million pities that Norcross had not comprehended the danger that lay in leaving that scummy, oozing mass undisturbed — but, be it said in his favour, his main concern had been a sample. At the time he had not thought of anything else.

So, hour after hour, into the long summer evening, grey streaks formed, broke up, evolved rapidly into individual Slitherers, and then they had shot northward with the speed of a bullet. Their very method of flight was foreign to this world. No wings, no visible sign of propulsion. Just the power of terrific velocity, either vertically or horizontally. And as for sex — merely, as Adams had foreseen — the power of fission whereby the weird bodies split lengthwise and formed two smaller but nonetheless deadly creatures.

In all parts of England, on this particular evening, Slitherers were sighted, and wondered about. Some people had heard the early TV and radio reports; others were in the dark. Both classes were not particularly concerned. There did not seem to be anything to panic about in the sight of grey flashing shapes, sometimes high and sometimes low. Real horror only came when one of the creatures flashed into direct action and left an imbecile man or woman behind.

As the evening faded into mellow twilight reports of sudden horror and death began to come in to various police stations and hospitals. From Scotland to southern England calls for help came so thick and fast that it took the police all their time to keep up with them. Besides, they didn't know what they were tackling, and in most cases when they arrived on the scene of tragedy the Slitherer responsible for the damage had gone elsewhere.

In twos and threes, then in gradually increasing numbers, men and women became aware that the sunny countryside was no longer a safe place in which to be. Children too were warned not to wander too far from home . . . For that matter the night did not bring any relief either. Slitherers came through windows and down chimneys in search of their prey — always leaving behind the mindless and the dying. Here and there men and women hit back with whatever weapons they had handy, but the astounding toughness of the Slitherers made them hard to kill. More often than not they emerged as the victors.

And throughout this sinister evening, quite unaware of what was transpiring around him, Norcross spent his time in study. He gave a few relevant details to his puzzled wife, and left the rest to her imagination. The shake-up for him came when his wife listened to the late night television bulletin, and promptly transferred the news to him as he sat in the back room, poring over books.

'Those horrible things have been at it again, Hartley,' she told him urgently. 'Some of them have been killed and I've just seen them . . . ' His wife finished with a shudder.

'Seen them?' Norcross repeated sharply. 'Where?'

'On the telly, of course. Some of the things have been slain and a telecamera was rushed to the scene. I never saw anything so ghastly in my life. It's — it's eerie somehow. Like something you read about but which could never happen.'

'It's happening all right,' Norcross said grimly, 'and as far as I can see it will go on happening — at least for the moment. Folks will have to combat it as best they can.'

His wife came closer to him, kneeling on the pouffe beside the armchair.

'I think you know more than you're telling, Hartley. What are they? What are they doing here?'

He shook his head. 'I can't answer either question, Lucy. I certainly don't know what they are, nor what they're driving at. Offhand, crazy though it is, it seems that the whole business began because a girl carried meat paste sandwiches.'

His wife pouted. 'That doesn't *start* to make sense.'

'Don't I know it! When the Ministry asked me to investigate giant corn I didn't know what I was going to get into. Back of my mind is the thought all the time that these things belong to another world, and got here by some accident or other. If we were placed accidentally on another world we'd fight everything, wouldn't we, in order to protect ourselves? I fancy these Slitherers are doing the same thing.'

'You don't suggest that these vile creatures are the inhabitants of another world, do you? If so I certainly don't want to see that world.'

'I don't suggest they are the thinking race of another planet, but some low order thereof. Just as though some of the Earthly tarantula transported to another planet would not represent our thinking race called man ... Now be a dear and leave me alone. I've a lot to think out before resuming the investigation tomorrow.'

Lucy sighed and got to her feet. 'I just don't know what things are coming to,' she complained. 'What with rocket projectiles, satellites in space, flying saucers, and heaven knows what, there's no telling what — '

Norcross looked up sharply. 'Flying saucers!'

'That's what I said,' Lucy yawned, and shuffled back into the lounge again.

'Flying saucers,' Norcross repeated slowly. 'By God, I just wonder . . . '

He went over to the drawer in which, in manilla folders, he kept all the press cuttings concerning unusual scientific happenings — mainly as a hobby. Before long he came to a detailed report of the last known visit of flying saucers in March. Now it was July.

Carefully he read — and then re-read. Finally he picked up the telephone and rang the number of Adams, his fellow worker.

'Hello, there?' came Adams' voice

'Norcross here,' Norcross said. 'Look,

you can think me crazy if you like, but it can't be any more crazy than the rest of this business ... How about flying saucers? They were here in strength in March last.'

'Agreed. What about it?'

'According to the report I have here, several of the saucers trailed a smoke-screen — in every country of the world. At least we *thought* it was a smoke-screen, but supposing it wasn't? Let us suppose the mist was something else.'

'All right. What was it then?'

'Suppose it was the unknown element which we've discovered in the fertilizer? Not smoke at all but a fine powder of some sort?'

Silence. Plainly Adams was pondering.

'It ties up,' Norcross continued, with a quiet insistence. 'The wheat was not gigantic in just one field, but in every part of the world. Remember the conferences to decide on market prices for the stuff? The saucers were also in every part of the world. I think there's only one conclusion to be drawn from it all — that the saucers disseminated some kind of stuff, a brownish powder, so fine that it looked like smoke as it came down, and which was more or less invisible when it fell on the soil. It has some mystic property to promote gigantic plant growth. It got mixed up with ordinary fertilizer because nobody knew what it was, and there was no reason to suspect anything. That is why the fertilizer I got from Coxwold is contaminated with this unknown element of which the manufacturers know nothing.'

'Yes, sounds logical,' Adams agreed. 'But whoever heard of a plant food — if that's what it is — being selective? What possessed it to solely stimulate wheat growth and leave everything else untouched?'

Norcross smiled faintly. 'As yet, old man, agricultural science on earth is one of the youngest sciences. There are thousands of things yet to be discovered. A race which has perfected flying saucers might conceivably have also perfected marvellous plant foods which are intensely selective in that they react only to certain kinds of plants — in this case wheat.'

'Mmmm, it sticks together so far — except for the very obvious question mark. Why? Where's the sense in just stimulating our wheat fields, and what has that to do with the Slitherers?'

'I don't know yet; but if we have the answer to part of the puzzle it's a safe bet that we'll get the rest of it. Somehow, the brown ingredient in the fertilizer, the composition of some meat paste sandwiches, and the Slitherers, are all mixed up — and definitely interconnected. There's another point too. The source of the Slitherers is in Coxwold, where the meat sandwiches fell. In no other part of the world, even though brown mystery powder has presumably fallen there, is there any mention of Slitherers — so it seems an inescapable fact that the meat paste had something to do with it.'

'Seems like it. All right, what are we going to do?'

'As I said, I had thought of visiting the fertilizer manufacturers tomorrow, but in the face of this new theory I don't think it would do much good. I'll visit the manufacturers of the meat paste instead. Before then, I'll trace this girl who had the sandwiches and find out whose brand of meat paste it was . . . What's her name now? Rita Haslam. I can trace her through the newspapers. Okay — I'll see you at the lab some time tomorrow.'

With that Norcross rang off and, keeping to his plan, he spent another half hour tracing the address of Rita Haslam through the newspaper which had fully published her story. This done, he paid a late call upon her for, fortunately, she lived at a not very great distance. Her parents were obviously puzzled by Norcross's advent, and listened in silent perplexity to his questions.

'I'm sorry to revive an incident which must have unpleasant memories for you, Miss Haslam,' Norcross apologised, 'but the facts you may be able to give me will help a lot . . . I believe you had meat paste sandwiches about the time your — er — boy friend was attacked by Slitherers?'

Rita shuddered a little at the memory of the incident, but she nonetheless held herself well in control.

'Actually the business with the meat sandwiches was some time before, Mr.

71

Norcross. It was about a week before the actual attack of the Slitherers that I dropped those sandwiches — some of them anyway.'

'A week before, eh? Mmm, very interesting. How did it happen exactly?'

'I went to retrieve a carelessly flung mineral bottle and, in stooping, some of my sandwiches slipped out of the parcel.'

'And you didn't pick any of them up?'

'All covered with plant fertilizer? Not likely!'

A gleam came in Norcross's eye. 'They were covered in fertilizer, you say?'

'Definitely!'

'Thank you . . . About this meat paste. Whose brand was it?'

'Er — ' Rita thought for a moment. 'I don't know. I didn't make up the sandwiches.'

'I did,' her mother said, still puzzled. 'It was a jar of Selby's turkey paste. I've used it for years.'

'Selby's. Thanks a lot — '

'Mr. Norcross,' interjected the girl's father, 'what is all this questioning about? Are you a detective, or something?'

Norcross shrugged. 'I suppose I am in a way. Professionally, I am a chemist, working for the Ministry of Agriculture. I don't need to tell you how serious this business of the Slitherers has become and I'm collecting every available fact about them.'

'But what have Rita's meat sandwiches got to do with it?'

'More than you, Rita, or anybody imagines,' Norcross said slowly. 'However, don't for a moment think you are in any kind of trouble, Miss Haslam,' he added. 'You dropped your sandwiches by accident, and started something unbelievable — and horrible. Come to think of it, meat paste is not the correct term. Poultry paste would be better.'

'All sounds crazy to me,' the girl's father grunted.

'Crazy? Yes, maybe you're right. I think it would be more correct to say — a scientific accident . . . Er, Miss Haslam, at the risk of harrowing you again, how exactly did your boy friend look when he staggered out to meet you after being attacked by the Slitherers?'

'He — he looked like a mental deficient,' Rita replied, hesitating. 'He walked like a blind man, kind of feeling his way, and those horrible giant tadpoles, or whatever they are, were clinging to his forehead and temples like leeches. Harry just couldn't brush them off.'

'And a short time afterwards he died?' Norcross asked quietly; and as the girl nodded miserably he got to his feet.

'That all?' asked her father, also rising.

'From me, yes,' Norcross agreed, 'but I think all of us are going to hear a lot more about the Slitherers before we're through. Thanks for the information you've given me, and I'm sorry to have taken up so much of your time.'

Thoughtfully Norcross made his way back home and in general he spent a pretty sleepless night thinking things over — but at least he evolved some plan of action out of the chaos and the next morning — full of the newspaper and radio and TV news of what had happened in the night — he paid an early visit to the city headquarters of Selby's, the meat paste and tinned food manufacturers.

Norcross was satisfied with no less a person than the laboratory manager, and this individual listened in rather puzzled but polite silence as Norcross explained.

'Is there something wrong with our turkey paste Mr. Norcross?' he asked at last.

'Nothing at all, far as I know. I simply want the exact formula.'

'I gathered that, but I'm in no position to give it without the consent of the Board of Directors. Don't you realize that all of our foods are protected by patent, and — '

'I know that, but there is I believe — some ingredient or other in your turkey paste which is the answer to the mysterious Slitherers which are terrifying the country. Naturally you've heard of them?'

'Of course, but how you can assume that our turkey paste is connected with them is beyond me.'

Norcross's long nose twitched but he did not lose his temper.

'I have to put it clearly to you, sir. Either I have the full formula, or I shall reluctantly be compelled to ask the Ministry of Agriculture to enforce it.'

'What has the Ministry of Agriculture got to do with turkey paste? Answer me that!'

Norcross did answer it, in full. Altogether he was nearly an hour getting what he wanted, and even then the Managing Director had to be cajoled into giving his blessing — but Norcross came out with the formula and a satisfied grin on his inquisitive face . . . He had lunch, and then put in a belated appearance at the laboratory.

'Chief wants you,' were Adams' first words.

'Oh, hell!' Norcross turned round and went out again. In a moment or two he had entered the office of the laboratory director.

'Oh, there you are, Norcross. I suppose you've heard the latest news about these things called the Slitherers?'

'Last I heard of them they were attacking people right, left, and centre.'

'Exactly, and up to an hour ago they were still breeding down in Coxwold.

That's why I sent for you. You were supposed to be looking into the Coxwold business. How far have you got?'

'Did you say 'up to an hour ago' the Slitherers were still breeding? What's happened since then?'

'By now,' the laboratory director said complacently, 'all the breeding ground will have been destroyed. I got permission to send an army detachment down to Coxwold. Since the place has been evacuated anyway it would be all right to destroy the cornfield with small bombs — and incidentally the Slitherers' breeding ground. I'm expecting a call announcing success at any moment. The point is, Norcross: what are you supposed to be doing?'

Briefly, Norcross gave the details of his activities to date. The director listened in silence.

'You are pursuing an unusual course, Norcross. However, the assignment was put in your hands, so work it out in your own way — but don't be too long about it. The public is wanting to know something. Consequently the Government has got its own scientists to work as well to tackle the business. If you can, we want to score a success, eh Norcross?'

'Matter of fact, sir, I don't think it signifies just as long as we stamp the trouble out.'

'In that case the army will take the credit. With the breeding grounds destroyed the rest is easy.'

'Easy?' Norcross raised an eyebrow. 'I don't think so, sir. The Slitherers that have already been born are our real trouble. Since they increase their numbers by dividing themselves there is no limit to their numbers. Destroying the Coxwold field is merely a classic example of shutting the stable door after the horse has gone.'

For a moment the director looked annoyed that his genius should be questioned; then he picked up the telephone as it shrilled.

'Walsingham here. What is it?' Then he sat listening intently. Finally his expression changed to dumbfounded amazement. 'It couldn't happen, man! It couldn't!'

More fast talking on the line, which Norcross could not catch.

'All right,' Walsingham said at last, dazed. 'Yes — do what you like. Use tanks if you have to — or contact the Air Ministry and have the area bombed — Yes, yes of course I have Government sanction.'

Slowly he put the 'phone down again and then met the eyes of Norcross across the desk.

'Astounding thing!' he declared. 'That detachment of the militia which went down to Coxwold has been wiped out! All fifty of them! Before they could even get into position they were attacked by the Slitherers and, after brief mindless wandering, collapsed and died. There's absolute panic down there.'

Norcross rubbed his chin. 'That sounds as though the Slitherers must have returned in force to Coxwold for some reason. Did I understand you to say that the air force was going to be used next?'

'Only way, isn't it?'

'I suppose so, sir,' Norcross agreed. 'Anyway, my angle on all this is different, as you'll realise. I'll get along to the lab and see what more I can find out.'

'Yes, do that — and let me know how you get on.'

Norcross wasted no time in returning to his own department, where he drew Adams on one side from the general laboratory staff. In a matter of moments he had briefed him in what was happening to date.

'So now it's a matter of what?' Adams asked.

'We've got first to work out this turkey paste formula and then see what its relationship is to the unknown ingredient in the fertilizer. Let's see now — There's still some of that unknown ingredient locked away in the fridge from my first experiment. We can work on that . . . Come to think of it, we'd better have a jar of Selby's turkey paste, too. Hop out and get one, will you?'

Norcross handed over some money and then pulled from his jacket the formula he had extracted from Selby's. He read it over as he changed into the smock.

'Dextrone,' he repeated finally, after summing up the other ingredients and finding them normal enough. 'What the blazes is dextrone?'

He frowned over it for a moment, then crossed to the monthly sheet of the latest substances legally permitted for use by the Government. Casting back to the April sheet he found 'dextrone' listed as a substance altogether suitable for human consumption, and apparently one of the gelatin brigade. In brief, in the case of the turkey paste, it had been used — and was still being used — as a binding ingredient in place of the usual gelatin.

Norcross sat down and reflected. By no possible process could the other ingredients of the turkey paste cause any kind of trouble, but the dextrone was another matter. A newly discovered substance, produced originally from animal matter, as are all the gelatin substances . . .

Then Adams came in with the pot of turkey paste. Norcross nodded, unscrewed the lid, and sniffed at the contents.

'We might make sandwiches, go on a picnic, and forget the whole thing,' Adams grinned — but at Norcross's stony look he fell silent.

'This is no joking matter, Adams. It's

dam' serious, believe me.' Norcross fished some of the turkey meat paste out of the jar with a spatula. 'You've heard of dextrone, you say?'

'Only vaguely. Had to do with it last week, as a matter of fact. It's an extract of gelatin used both in food and explosives.'

'Bright boy. Anyway, this stuff is bound with it instead of the usual gelatin. Our job is to isolate it.'

Which to an analytical chemist was not a serious problem. In half an hour isolation from the turkey paste proper was complete and the two men stood looking at the pale yellow jelly substance pensively.

'A product of bones, cartilage, and other substances,' Norcross said slowly. 'Summed up, the product of an animal. Now let's see what is the affinity for the mysterious something in the fertilizer.'

He opened the refrigerator and looked first at the tin he had placed there the previous night. It looked exactly the same, its contents frosted over. Then he removed the unknown grey-brown dust — contained in a small jar — which he had placed there at the close of his former unsuccessful analysis. Pondering, he came over to the bench.

'Mix these two together and things ought to happen as before,' he said, ladling some of the brown dung onto the bench. 'Let's see.'

Into the percentage of dung he mixed some of the dextrone, but nothing happened. Just a sticky brown mess like paste, which showed not the least evidence of the unusual.

'Something missing,' Norcross said disappointed; then Adams glanced around and snapped his fingers.

'Sunlight maybe. Things seem to rely on that.'

Norcross nodded and moved the whole issue into line with sunlight streaming through the nearest window. Without doubt things were hot enough, but still nothing happened.

'Very queer. Very queer indeed,' Norcross muttered. 'Surely it wasn't some odd co-incidence that happened once and will never happen again for thousands of years?' For a moment or two he was mystified, then he looked up sharply. 'I've got it! Most of the sun's important radiations are blocked by ordinary window glass — ultra violet for one, and there may be others. We did the last job in *undiluted* sunlight. Right! Pull that cardboard from the smashed pane.'

Adams obeyed and a cool breeze came floating into the laboratory. Norcross shifted the mess to be in the clear sunlight and then watched intently. The stuff showed signs now of becoming more jellified than before, proving it was not warmth alone which affected it. Then, abruptly, streaks of grey like cigarette ash . . . Norcross gave a yelp and whirled the lot into the waste bin. As before he put a stop to trouble with a good dose of acid.

'Well, that's that,' he said, rubbing his eyebrow. 'It would seem that the dextrone and the unknown brown substance have an affinity for each other, and that affinity is only complete when unmasked sunshine is at work. It isn't the heat that causes things to happen; it is something in the radiations of the sun, and ordinary window glass blocks the radiations . . . So far, so good. What we have got to do is analyse this brown substance again, though God knows I've tried every trick.'

Just the same Norcross went to work again, this time extending the field of activity so as to include the electron-microscope. With this instrument in operation he and Adams stood looking at the brown substance, now immensely magnified.

'In some ways it looks like rope; in others like a chain of variously shaped objects. Say a mineral string. Even analysed down to the limit like this the brown stuff doesn't tell us anything.'

'Dextrone might,' Norcross mused, and since the electron-microscope was in range of the sunlight from the broken window he added a trace of dextrone to the brown substance and watched intently.

It was not long before things happened. The vari-shaped pieces in the mass of brown substance twitched as the dextrone flowed viscidly into their midst. Slowly the brown chain broke up, each unit assuming a queer life of its own and gradually turning grey in the process.

'We've got it,' Adams whispered. 'This is *it*!'

Norcross did not answer. He was too busy studying the phenomenon taking place before his eyes, and under the intense power of the microscope it was possible to see the grey shapes change from mere specks of living matter into a decided outline — the embryonic formation of a Slitherer . . . Before things got out of hand Norcross switched off, removed the stuff from the microscope, and once again rid himself of it by use of acid.

'You're a biologist,' he said at last, looking at Adams. 'What ideas have you got?'

'Incredible ones, I'm afraid. It looked to me as though the brown stuff is actually living matter, only it doesn't behave like it until it has the dextrone working on it.'

'My idea too, which seems to suggest that the dextrone is, in some way, a catalyst.'

The two men were silent for a moment, aware that they were coming to the deep waters.

'The brown stuff is not affected by 'naked' sunlight alone,' Norcross resumed thoughtfully. 'It has lain in the fields for long enough under this fierce summer sunlight without doing anything more than cause a tremendous wheat crop in every part of the world. Yet the moment it gets accidentally mixed up with dextrone things start to happen and it changes from fertilizer — which we will assume is its basic nature — into a cradle of horror. Why?'

'That we don't know,' Adams said sensibly. 'Nobody can ever predict what a catalyst will do. For that matter, nobody really knows what a catalyst is. It just happens to be something that produces a certain effect on something else, as in this case.'

'From which it is logical to infer that no menace was intended — that whoever sent the brown fertilizer in the first place had no intention of creating Slitherers which would endanger our security.'

'It looks that way,' Adams admitted. 'From which I gather you are still clinging to your original idea that the flying saucers last March were responsible for the brown fertilizer?'

Norcross shrugged. 'Have you any other ideas to explain how the stuff created giant wheat all over the world?'

'No, afraid I haven't,' Adams confessed; then he frowned. 'But assuming you're right, why should the people of another planet wish to improve on our wheat?'

'No idea. Certainly the stuff worked since it functioned in every wheat field in the world — then came this catalyst in the form of meat paste and a bountiful harvest turned into tragedy, a tragedy which as yet has not been mastered.'

'I hope,' Adams said bitterly, 'that the aliens are satisfied with their handiwork!'

Norcross still clung to the logic of the situation. 'Unless they have taken close-hand observations from a flying saucer without our knowing it, they can't possibly have any intimation of what is happening ... More's the pity. They might have something to counteract it.'

'So now where are we?' Adams asked, moving restlessly. 'To prove that no menace was intended doesn't make the menace any the less real. What's to be done? There may be tens of thousands of Slitherers in various parts of the world by this time, and they can increase ad infinitum.'

Norcross did not seem to be listening. His eyes had the far-away look of a man thinking deeply.

'Chemically, with regard to this brown fertilizing element, we are forced to one definite conclusion. It contains life force of an obscure kind, and therefore in the normal way is capable of transmitting that life force to plants, as indeed in a very rudimentary way do some of our plant foods. The trouble comes when a catalyst breaks up the life force into cells, which in turn evolve rapidly into living creatures . . . '

'But why the gargantuan wheat?' Adams asked.

'We can only guess.' Norcross shrugged. 'Perhaps the home planet of these aliens is much further from its sun than the Earth from our sun. Hence this plant food from another planet has acted with tremendous force on wheat under the hot

Earth sun, probably far and away in excess of anything on this other world. For that we have to thank the warmth of the sun. The Slitherers are a different matter, even though the sun is again the major factor. But it is not the warmth in that case: it is something in the radiations that completes the — the circuit of life, as it were.'

Adams came to a stop in his pacing. 'We have the devil of a lot to take for granted,' he said. 'We can only form conclusions from our own investigations, and the rest is a mystery. We don't know — and probably never shall know — why the aliens decided our wheat crop needed stimulating, but we do know that we've got to be rid of these Slitherers, and as quickly as possible. What's the answer?'

'That's hardly our problem,' Norcross shrugged. 'The Government is deciding how best to be rid of the things, using the army and air force. As far as I can see our own part in the investigation is at an end. We have drawn all the conclusions we can . . . '

'Officially, yes — but for our own

satisfaction we ought to find out a good deal more. What are the Slitherers aiming at, for instance? Presumably they are a new form of life — even new to these aliens — so what is their objective? Plain killing for killing's sake?'

'Apparently. And yet — ' Norcross became silent, stroking his long nose. He was thinking back on Rita Haslam's remarks and a frown slowly settled.

'My God!' he said at length, awe-struck by the nature of his own speculations.

'What?'

'I was just thinking . . . In every case these Slitherers have struck at the head — usually the forehead — and they have left behind imbeciles who have died shortly afterwards. The forehead! That's the most likely place to attack if the brain is the objective. In the majority of cases the hair of the individual would prevent these things getting a hold on other parts of the head. The only exception would be a bald-headed man.'

'Well?'

'Can it be that these things are capable of drawing *intelligence* out of a person?

That they leave imbeciles behind seems to suggest that is what they do. Leeches, man! They have the quality of leeches, but where they draw blood these things perhaps draw intellect — and if they do that they must be becoming more intelligent with every person they attack.'

Adams was not stampeded, but he was certainly shocked at this new aspect of the problem.

'They have revealed a certain amount of intelligence already,' Norcross went on. 'Take the case of the army detachment who tried to eliminate them. What happened? The Slitherers congregated in the spot where they were originally born and — *anticipated* them, so accurately indeed that they slew the enemy first!'

'It hangs together,' Adams admitted, biting his lip. 'But is it possible to draw intelligence out of anybody? Isn't it too vague a quality to be absorbed by material means?'

'No reason why it should be. Brain emanations — which one might call thoughts — are measurable on instruments. Those emanations could surely be absorbed by an organism capable of receiving them. If the Slitherers have some kind of physical composition able to retain the brain emanations they have absorbed then they will make use of the knowledge they have literally sucked from their victims. For all we know their structure may be entirely a mass of neurones and fibres similar to that of a brain itself.'

'And yet lowly enough to divide themselves by fission?' Adams questioned doubtfully. 'The two things don't tally.'

'Then maybe division in their case is not of quite such a lowly order as we think. It may be their natural sex reaction. Remember we're dealing with something never experienced before.'

'If these things are absorbing intelligence with each man, woman, child or animal they kill,' Adams said slowly, 'the danger is increased a thousand fold, because the more intelligent they become the more difficult will they be to destroy . . . '

'I think,' Norcross said, 'that in spite of the risk we're taking we'll create a Slitherer from that jelly in the fridge and then kill it. After that we'll dissect.'

'Neither of us is very much up in that art,' Adams objected.

'Maybe not, but we've enough common knowledge to be able to recognise the interior structure of a Slitherer when we've cut it open. Right! We'll do that.'

By this time the two men had lost all track of time, so absorbed were they in their work. Actually it was nearing lunchtime, a matter that could hardly have interested them less at the moment, until a thought suddenly struck Norcross as he glanced at the clock.

'We'll hold it over until the rest of them go for lunch,' he said, nodding towards the staff. 'Then if there is any danger they won't be involved in it.'

Adams nodded a trifle uneasily and for the rest of the time until lunch he and Norcross discussed again the various aspects of the problem, without arriving at any new conclusion. Only when the last of the laboratory staff had departed did Norcross bring the tin of 'jelly' into view and surveyed the frost fronds with which it was caked.

'Better leave it in the sun to thaw out,' he said, setting it down in front of the nearest window. 'Then we'll be ready for whatever happens.'

Adams looked at the broken window, a little further away. 'Ought you not to let *direct* sun shine on it?'

'No. That's only necessary to create the actual things in the first place, when we have the fusion of dextrone and fertilizer. Once that is done with warmth does the rest ... As it is doing now,' Norcross finished, nodding to the grey streaks that had appeared in the gummy mess.

So, within an incredibly short space of time, several Slitherers took form, first in the 'tadpole' stage, then growing swiftly into eel-like formation. In this particular streak of weird living grey substance there were as many as six Slitherers, with other grey streaks commencing to form.

'Right,' Norcross said finally, his voice tense with excitement. 'This one's big enough.'

He singled out the largest and, using a pair of long-handled stainless steel tongs, he lifted the almost full grown object out of the jelly that had been its birthplace and placed it on the bench. It lay motionless, apparently orientating itself to the situation.

'Put the others in the fridge,' Norcross ordered, and Adams promptly obeyed, thankfully closing the refrigerator door. Then he turned back to Norcross who was in the act of filling a hypodermic with lethal fluid.

'This ought to kill it stone dead, yet at the same time not burn or destroy any of its organs,' he said. 'Here goes.'

Not knowing any particular part of the reptilian anatomy to select he took a chance and drove the needle in at random. The Slitherer reared up instantly in violent reaction, the hypodermic projecting like a miniature harpoon from its body. Instantly Norcross sprang back and darted for the laboratory door with Adams immediately behind him. There, with the door ajar in case a sudden dash were needed, they watched what happened.

Not for long, however. The 'harpooned' Slitherer darted in various directions at lightning speed, apparently not at all sure what it was doing. Certainly the co-ordination that had been noticeable in previous creatures was not evident in this one . . . Then the poison must have taken effect for, in darting for a huge bottle on which to rest, its flight suddenly faltered and it dropped to the floor.

For a second or two it lashed furiously, then very gradually movement ceased and it became still.

'Okay,' Norcross murmured. 'I think we've done it.'

He and Adams moved forward to investigate. There was no doubt that the thing was well and truly dead, its murderous little eyes already glazing and its body beginning to stiffen. Unceremoniously Norcross slapped it on the bench and withdrew the hypodermic. Then he went over to an instrument cupboard and came back with two very sharp knives.

'Do your best,' he said to Adams. 'It needn't be a perfect surgical job — in fact it *won't* be. All we need is to cut it open like filleting a fish, and then examine it.'

This did not present any great difficulty.

The queer, rubbery flesh of the Slitherer gave way quickly enough under the knives, and considering they were not skilled workers the two men made a fairly good job of their task. In the end they had two rough halves, which they stood and looked at interestedly.

'Main vertebrae anyhow,' Norcross said, indicating it. 'After which it branches off into these myriads of hinged side bones, somewhat after the structure of an eel. Apparently this watery stuff is the equivalent of its blood. Now, its internal organs and nervous system . . . '

For this the ordinary microscope was called into action, and the whole business was mainly Adams' field as a biologist. In the end he looked up at Norcross.

'Your guess was a mighty good one,' he said. 'Its body structure, apart from the main hinged bone framework, is a complicated mass of criss-crossing ganglia and nerves, together with filigrees of finer nervous tissue. The thing is a highly sensitive living receiver of impressions, and as such a perfect creature for picking up weak impulses of brain frequencies.'

'So far, so good,' Norcross said, nodding. 'The thing could store brain impulses and utilize them. We've discovered that much. Now something else: what makes it have such strange powers of propulsion and such terrific speed?'

This was a problem difficult to pinpoint, but the answer seemed to lie in an organ close to the Slitherer's tail, an organ which had a small channel leading from it to a pair of lips on the outside of its body.

'I think the answer lies here,' Adams said, 'but what the answer is I wouldn't know. We can, however, hazard a guess . . . Plainly, a creature which can absorb brain frequencies must have a mainly electrical constitution, so why not an electrical method of propelling itself? Even creatures in our own animal kingdom, and fish kingdom, have many electrical tendencies. We can assume that this one, perhaps, utilizes in some electrical way the lines of magnetic force that exist between all material objects. They do exist, and machines can prove it, but nobody has ever attempted to turn them to account. Perhaps the Slitherers do it naturally. After all, lines of force exist as much on other planets as they do here, if these creatures have ever reached the adult stage elsewhere.'

Norcross nodded slowly. 'Okay, we'll accept the line of magnetic force as the only one we can think of. Not that it matters too much, though I'd like to know what makes them tick. What does stand out is that they're capable of being absorbers of intelligence to an amazing degree, and for that reason the danger they represent is appalling.'

They were both silent for a moment, rather surprised that they had discovered so much. Then presently Norcross stirred.

'I'll make out a report on our findings to date and let the chief have it. Maybe other biologists and scientists will check our findings and have a few bright suggestions to offer. Far as I can see right now we've done all we can . . . We'll put this thing in the fridge for future use — if any — and then go and hunt up some lunch.'

4

Massacre

Such is human nature that, despite all they had learned about the Slitherers, Norcross and Adams did not go to any outrageous lengths to pursue their enquiries still further. They had beyond doubt solved most of the problem, but there they stopped without doing anything more. Which was a pity. If they had had the wit to go back to the Coxwold wheat field, for instance, they would have seen that the jelly mass of dextrone and brown fertilizer was still producing dozens of Slitherers an hour, always from the same mass of stuff. Naturally, no outsider knew that the mass seemed to be eternal in its productive capacity because they hadn't got the least inkling of what was going on.

Actually, there lay in the brown fertilizer mixed with the dextrone, countless millions of eggs, far too minute for the human eye to see, and only brought to fruition by the sun's radiations and warmth. As one lot of eggs broke up into the first cellular organism that later became a Slitherer, yet another lot took its place. Inexhaustible, as long as the catalyst of the dextrone was in action. Had the dextrone-fertilizer mass been exterminated to the last drop the Slitherers would have stopped — except for those which were already in existence — but the importance of doing this never occurred to anybody, except perhaps Norcross and Adams and they considered the matter out of their hands.

The air force under Government orders duly bombed the Coxwold field and reduced it to a mass of craters and smoke — which was about as much use as hurling a brick into a mass of table jelly. The stuff was blasted out of its original position, certainly, but thousands of little pieces simply scattered under impact and dropped into more brown fertilizer, since every part of the ground was covered with it. So instead of destroying the seat of the trouble the high and mighty air force only succeeded in creating hundreds more . . . The Coxwold field still thrived as the cradle of Slitherers, and the hot, unclouded weather aided the process.

It was a curious thing, but the Slitherers, through some kind of intuition, seemed to know that the Coxwold field was their birthplace. Vast numbers of them — perhaps all of them — returned from wide perigrinations to the Coxwold field every night, a fact which first became evident to the pilot of a low flying 'plane who, one evening, happened to fly across Coxwold as a short cut to his air base. He reported the fact, and the high-ups considered the matter — and still considered it. And considered it again. And Coxwold meanwhile was becoming one of the deadliest places on Earth.

From press, radio, and television, it was evident that the Slitherers were not confining themselves to England. After a time there were reports of them appearing in America, Europe, Canada, Asia — in fact all over the globe. There became established such a daily list of killings by the creatures that the public accepted them as phlegmatically as the road accident figures. Something had come into public life which apparently could not be side-stepped, and that was all there was to it.

Until, by degrees, a voice here and there raised itself in protest — voices that mattered, such as the Primate of England, the President of the United States, and others. The constant carnage from flying, slithering horrors that struck by night and day had got to be stamped out somehow. It was no longer a matter of accepting it: it was time to do something.

But what? The air force chiefs insisted, perhaps rightly, that they could not possibly chase the horrors and eliminate them. For one thing there were too many of them, and for another they were never in the same place twice. Equally it was impossible to kill the things on land because one never knew where they would turn up next. And finally, even attacking the Coxwold field would not accomplish anything. It was the numbers abroad, and constantly on the increase, that presented the real problem.

Then on top of these troubles there descended yet another, which began with a mysterious disease. It commenced in England first, and then appeared in various other countries with equal malignancy. It seemed to be some kind of food poisoning that killed within twelve hours, and all the skill and scientific resources of the medical faculty failed to overcome the trouble.

It was at this point that Norcross felt he ought to say what he thought about the business — and he did so to the laboratory director.

'There's only one cure for this malady which is slowly killing everybody en masse,' he said frankly. 'Start a campaign ordering everybody to stop eating bread — or at any rate the bread made from the giant corn yields.'

The director looked surprised. 'What are you suggesting, Norcross?'

'I'm suggesting that in some way the corn is poisonous because of the fertilizer that has nourished it. Now the stuff is distributed throughout the world in the form of flour — and bread — the poison is noticeable . . . Doctors have admitted they can't find a cure for it, and that isn't surprising with the source of the poison belonging to another world.'

In his own mild way Norcross had spoken, and be it said to his credit, the laboratory director did not let it end there. He passed the news on to the right quarter, and to the press, and finally Government legislation came into force to prohibit the sale of bread indefinitely. What stocks there were, and the flour too, were to be destroyed, save certain percentages retained for analysis . . . In this last capacity Norcross came into his own, and because of his prior experience in the matter he was appointed as Director during the emergency, with Adams as his right hand man.

'I cannot believe,' he told a gathering of scientists and general technicians at the Agriculture laboratories, 'that the thing we face has been deliberately engineered, gentlemen. I think it is all a gigantic accident without any intention of trying to destroy our civilization — but the fact does remain that in our little band of workers there is centred the hopes of all civilization. A big thought, gentlemen, yet true nevertheless . . . We have no special knowledge of what we are fighting. What we *do* know of this menace is mainly the outcome of inference — but one fact is clear. Unless we destroy the Slitherers as thoroughly as we are destroying the products of our world cornfields, civilization itself will come crashing down. Earth will be populated by a race of darting grey demons who are born destroyers and nothing else.'

'At the latest report,' said one of the technicians, 'there are something like twenty thousand known Slitherers in being, and increasing steadily day by day.'

'Exactly, and they will go on increasing by natural sexual process — but there wouldn't have been so many if the original breeding ground had been systematically and completely wiped out. That job was *bungled*, which is why there are so many Slitherers to deal with.'

'We can't stop the sexual increase going on, but we can and will smash the Coxwold field breeding ground as a start and so prevent thousands on thousands more of the creatures being born. That is one of our first tasks.'

'How?' somebody asked. 'We've tried everything, including bombs and flame throwers.'

'There's one quite obvious thing which has not been tried, and I know it is effective from experience — nitric acid. Thousands of gallons of nitric acid must be unloaded onto the Coxwold field, and for an area for miles around it. That way the original jelly plasma that is the Slitherers' cradle will be destroyed, and all fragments of it that there may be in outlying areas . . . Then we will tackle the problem of how to dispose of the Slitherers themselves.'

And, since he had absolute authority to deal with the emergency, Norcross wasted no time. The air ministry was contacted and special planes were assigned to the task of attacking the Coxwold field. Within twenty-four hours the area of the field, and for five miles around, was deluged with nitric acid, leaving behind a soaking, smoking, blackened mass in which nothing of an organic nature could possibly live ... Later came the investigation, and the report that not a trace of 'Slitherer jelly' remained. The source of the trouble had been wiped out, but the greater problem still remained.

Once again, with his experts from every field of science, Norcross went to work. But this time he produced nothing out of the bag, no innovation that could get round the difficulty. It defied imagination to deal with thousands of unknown, multiplying horrors striking where, and when, they chose.

'You still believe these things are a product of another world, Mr. Norcross?' one of the technicians asked, in a brooding interval.

'Everything seems to point to it. But it is possible that the things have never appeared anywhere before in their present form. I think the radiations of the sun have something to do with them being alive at all.'

'Or just one particular radiation?' the technician asked. 'One which reaches Earth, but is not present on some other planet, either because of its distance from its primary or because of its atmospheric makeup?'

Norcross shrugged. 'I should think the radiation is as prevalent elsewhere as it is here. And remember the radiation is only operative at the actual birth of the Slitherers. That no longer obtains since we have destroyed the catalyst-produced amalgam.'

'Pity,' the technician signed. 'I was thinking that we might commence an analysis of the sun's various radiations in an effort to find the one which stimulates these Slitherers.'

'He may have something there,' one of the other men said. 'Every form of life evolves because of some radiation or other — usually solar. If these things rely on a particular solar wavelength, we might find a way of preventing them getting it.'

'How?' Norcross asked bluntly. 'Throw the sun into eclipse, or something? Do that, and every other form of life would also be wiped out. Can't be done. Forget it.'

And so the men argued round the table, trying this and that theory and invariably discarding it until presently Norcross came out with a suggestion, the only possible one under the circumstances.

'As I see it, there is only one way. People must themselves form into vigilantes — small groups with a leader — and they must take action against every Slitherer in their area. They must be fully armed for the purpose, of course. In that way, with groups all over the world, it should be possible to gradually exterminate the pests.'

'In theory, yes,' another agreed, 'but what about the vast areas of Earth that are unpopulated, where Slitherers abound? How is one to get at those regions?'

'One can't,' Norcross said, 'but it isn't those regions which matter. It's the civilized parts that must be defended, and I think my method is the only one, at least for the time being . . . While the Vigilantes protect immediate interests we'll work out something else.'

'Such as?'

'Find something lethal to the Slitherers,

but not to any other form of life. It won't be easy, but I'm sure it's possible. I'll make arrangements to have a live Slitherer sent to us and we'll experiment on it.'

So for the time being words gave place to action, and through press, radio, and television Norcross's idea of the Vigilantes was given pride of place, whilst in the background government heads went to work to authorise special weapons, and set up committees to supervise the issuing thereof. It was, declared the press, the biggest move forward yet to combat the mysterious invasion that was striking at the roots of civilization.

And, in the laboratories, with a specimen Slitherer sealed into a glass case and deliberately kept alive, Norcross and the scientists worked unceasingly to devise something or other that would kill the atrocity — and its fellows — without harming normal earthly life . . . Never was there a problem so gargantuan.

★   ★   ★

A million miles away in space a colossal space ship moved with easy velocity. For some five years it had pursued its journey from the vast reaches near Alpha Centauri; now it was in orbit around the Earth. For nearly six months it had pursued its present course, polarising screens effectively rendering it invisible to Earthly telescopes and radar.

Within its monstrous, radiation-proofed depths was almost an entire city, complete with every need. Those beings who manned the vessel knew exactly what was happening on Earth.

They were big and grave-faced, these last men and women of Alpha Centauri. They represented the highest intelligence of their race — a race whittled down to six hundred, the remnants of a once-mighty people.

Behind them, they had left a world suddenly overtaken by a poison gas outflow from Alpha Centauri, their sun. There had barely been time for them to get away. Intelligently, persistently, they were reaching out for a new world to inhabit — but forbearance and wisdom precluded the possibility that they should at any time secure their ends by violence.

Amongst them there was no air of viciousness, no satisfaction at the trouble harassing Earth. Rather, they were contrite.

'What has happened is not quite clear,' the leader Alphan said at length, after summing up the details. 'Certainly we have plunged the third world into turmoil and we can only hope, with their rather limited scientific accomplishments, that they will find a way to overcome the difficulty. If they do not, then it would seem that the third world will become denuded of life as it stands at present, and in its place will exist this unknown, vicious life which draws intelligence from its victims.'

'It would seem,' one of them remarked presently, 'that our experiment to discover if our fertilizer will work in Earthly conditions has taken on a malignant form. How, I ask, could FG9 — which is of course the perfect plant food — produce dangerous creatures like these?'

'That,' the leader Alphan responded, 'is

114

surely not such a big question, my friend? Our endeavour was to see if our FG9 fertilizer would operate on this planet's staple crop — which our observations had shown most closely approximated our own staple food, which we have brought with us — as it does on our own. If it had worked, then doubtless we could have come to some arrangement with this world's authorities for us to tenant the unused parts of their planet — amply sufficient for our small numbers — and in return for the concession hand them many of our scientific secrets. That was our main idea, the reason for our recent investigation of this planet's surface by our scout machines. Our inward journey through this system has shown that no other planet would suit us as well as this world's undeveloped areas, and we *had* to know how our crops would react under alien conditions, hence the FG spraying.'

The leader Alphan shook his head moodily. 'We know what has happened. The FG operated perfectly, at first, on this planet's closest equivalent to our own staple food, but it produces something in their crop that is fatal to their bodies, a factor we never foresaw. After that came the inimical creatures, produced by an accidental catalyst, which is causing untold trouble at this very moment. Since FG9 is a fertilizer composed of active minute life, the evolution of the creatures under a catalyst may not be deemed unusual. It has never happened to us because we have never encountered a catalyst . . . '

There was silence for a moment, then the leader Alphan concluded:

'And now? We can offer no help because the creatures are as much a mystery to us as to these people. They'll deal with them as best they can — but for us, all prospect of this world as a possible future habitat must be forgotten. After unintentionally creating crops which would have killed the populace if it had not been stopped promptly, and also sending fertilizer which has changed into malignant life, we would hardly be welcome.'

'Need we admit the responsibility?' one of the Alphans asked.

'Yes, my friend. We would not attempt to bargain whilst hiding some of the facts. That is not our way . . . We have failed in our endeavors, and we can only hope that, somehow, these people will survive the mortal blow we have accidentally dealt them . . . '

The leader fell silent, looking into the scanner at the weird spawning life they had brought about. Then he closed the switch that blanked the screen, and gave the order for their ship to leave the solar system and head for the next nearest star . . .

★ ★ ★

And while Norcross and his fellow scientists toiled untiringly to find a means of destroying the Slitherers, the darting demons themselves were in some curious kind of way getting themselves organised. Since there were something like 20,000 of them in being, and hundreds more being added daily, they were now in a position to cause a good deal of trouble, even more so since the intelligence they had gained from their victims was capable of being used. Further, the Slitherers had no human instincts with which to temper their desires. They were utterly without conscience and sentiment, seeing only with ever-increasing clearness that human beings were very much in the way of their own development.

The crystallisation of all this sub-human reasoning took shape in what was afterwards called the Burlinger massacre. Why Burlinger of all places happened to be chosen nobody knew, but the fact remained that this sleepy English village, drowsing in the warmth of the summer evening, experienced the first onslaught.

It happened just after seven o'clock, and it so happened that nearly all the populace of Burlinger — about 850 people — was on or around the green in the centre of the village. A vitally important cricket match was to be played, and there is nothing short of an earthquake that can stop a village cricket match.

So it was, then. The white flannelled players were out on the pitch; the obese umpire carried three hats and wore a dazzling overall. Old men and women lounged on forms with caps pulled down over their eyes; young men and women spooned in the quiet waters away from the general throng. Children careened around in various directions, more interested in their own pursuits than in cricket. And over it all, the perfect sleepy rustic scene, the late sun cast deep golden rays and slanting bars of shadow.

Then came the Slitherers, out of the cobalt blue of the northward sky, a solid mass of them, so close together they appeared at a distance as a fast rising cloud. The cricket umpire glanced up, muttered something to himself about a shower approaching — and then the whole cloud descended in a solid phalanx. There had never been anything like it before — never anything so savage, so merciless, or so perfectly timed.

Players, spectators, old and young, dogs and cats, even birds — the entire population of Burlinger disappeared under the cloud. In the space of five minutes the whole thing was over, and operating as one unit the Slitherers took to the air again satiated for the time being. They left behind a picture of still life, of men, women, and children scattered dead or dying on the green grass, of the white flanneled cricketers sprawled around the cricket pitch ... The sun's shadows lengthened and the church clock struck eight before a passing motorist came upon the astounding scene. It did not take him more than a few minutes to discover the bruised foreheads of the dead. He went direct to the police station, and the police notified the media. For the first time since the advent of the Slitherers, people the length and breadth of Britain really began to realise what they were up against.

And so did Norcross. Silent and grim-faced, tired from his day of fruitless experiments with his fellow scientists, he sat listening to the news, his knife and fork poised above his supper plate.

' . . . and the Government,' concluded the announcer, 'has tonight issued this emergency warning. People are advised, despite the hot weather, to bolt and bar all windows and doors at night, and where shutters are possible use those too. The Slitherers are not stopped by glass. Again, do not take walks through lonely country without a companion, and if possible arm yourselves with a walking stick, a poker, or any object that may help you beat off an attempted attack. As is already known, various cities and towns have set up their own armies of Vigilantes, armed with ammonia and acid guns. It is suggested that villages and hamlets should do the same, at least until the emergency is ended. Special booths will be set up as from tomorrow, in conjunction with local councils, for the distribution of Vigilante weapons . . . Finally, the late weather outlook: Continuing hot and sunny in all parts of England.'

Norcross switched off, then he tossed down his knife and fork and sat brooding. A moth drifted in through the open window and danced towards the table. It was the impact of his wife's hands coming together to exterminate it that jerked Norcross suddenly back into life.

121

'What a business that girl Rita Haslam started with her infernal turkey paste sandwiches,' he muttered. 'What a business! And we can see no end to it yet!'

'Try and eat your supper, dear,' Lucy urged. 'In spite of what's happened, you've got to go on living you know.'

Mechanically Norcross started eating. Then he paused again. 'It's becoming obvious that these devilish things are using intelligence now. Judging from the report of the Burlinger business the attack was perfectly planned, and co-ordinance was maintained throughout. Apparently the whole mass of the population were flattened and destroyed before they could do anything.'

'Yes . . . it looks like it,' Lucy Norcross agreed soberly,

'Suppose that had happened in a big town — at a rush hour, for instance, when big masses of people are congregated together.'

'It couldn't happen in a big town — '

'It could,' Norcross interrupted. 'And it even might, as the things become cleverer.' He took a few mouthfuls of food. 'Yes, things have taken a distinct turn for the worse. Earlier it was simply the haphazard victim anywhere, but now it is a mass attack on a chosen spot. Get a few more like that and panic will do the rest. Everything will be a shambles.'

Lucy looked out thoughtfully into the quiet twilight.

'Surely, surely there's something you and your colleagues can do? They're only reptiles after all, so why on earth should human beings be beaten by them?'

'Intelligent reptiles, my dear, which move at a terrific speed. Reptiles that fly: something that has never been in the world before. We don't know where they are going to attack, and they are as tough as the devil when we try to destroy them. Do you think we aren't trying to master the problem?'

'Yes. Yes, of course you are. I'm sorry, dear.'

Norcross put down his knife and fork and stretched out his hand. For a moment his long-nosed face was genuinely sympathetic.

'Sorry, Lucy, if I snapped. My nerves

are pretty well on edge — what with the hot weather, the Slitherers, and repeated failures. Not the best diet for a man with a load of responsibility — for sure enough there'll be a lot said to me tomorrow about this Burlinger business . . . ' He reflected. 'Y'know we've tried everything we can think of to deal with the Slitherers — electric currents, gas, vibration supersonic waves, the lot. We're trying to find a variation on one of those that will kill a Slitherer but not everything else as well. So far we've been unlucky.'

'What do you do then? Just keep on experimenting?'

'I suppose so — ' Norcross broke off and looked up sharply as a faint whirring noise, growing gradually louder, impressed itself upon him. After a moment he realised it was coming from somewhere outside, and he hurried quickly to the window. Quietly Lucy joined him. In silence they stood watching the twilit sky blacken with clouds of the flying horrors, moving at tremendous speed towards the south and making no effort to descend, as yet.

'Thousands of them — tens of

thousands!' Norcross whispered; then he turned and sped through the room and out of the back door. In the centre of the garden he stood looking up as cloud after cloud of the Slitherers swished with unbelievable velocity overhead at a height of perhaps a thousand feet,

'Either a terrific planned attack against somewhere or other,' Norcross murmured, as Lucy joined him again, 'or else they're going to roost . . . I never thought there were so many of them.'

'And still more!' Lucy said after a moment.

Norcross did not speak. In grimly puzzled silence he watched as four more clouds of the horrors came over, each cloud containing he knew not how many of the flying reptiles. Like those gone before these Slitherers made no attempt to descend or break formation. They kept on flying at their usual breathtaking speed, away to the south and slowly disappeared . . . As at last there seemed to be an end of them.

'Where can they be going if it isn't an attack on a city?' Norcross demanded;

then apparently struck with a thought he turned and headed into the house. Lucy watched him as he took down an atlas from the bookshelf. Spreading it open on the table he studied it.

'From the direction they were taking,' he said finally 'I'd say London was their objective, south from here. Beyond that we get into the southern counties and — '

'Coxwold,' Lucy put in. 'That's also in that direction. That's where they were born, isn't it?'

'Yes, but — Hmmm, wonder if you're right? We attacked their birthfield with acid, as you know and right now there's only a blackened waste remaining in Coxwold. I've never paid much attention to the place since we blasted it . . . Suppose the things return, by some sort of instinct — to their birthfield every night? Come back in formation, no matter where their day sojourns have taken them?'

He pondered the fact for a moment and then reached for the 'phone and called Adams' number. In a moment Adams himself responded.

'Prepared to take a risk, Adams?' Norcross asked. 'I think I've got a new angle on the Slitherers. Will you come over to Coxwold with me in the car?'

'Coxwold? Sure — but will it be any good at night?'

'The night's essential. All right, I'll pick you up in the car.'

Norcross folded the atlas up again and put it back on the shelf. His wife looked at him curiously.

'Not quite sure what I'm getting into,' he said, patting her arm, 'but for your sake I won't take any needless risks. Expect me when you see me.'

With that he was gone, and in fifteen minutes he had picked up Adams. Thereafter Norcross passed round the edge of London until he hit the main road to the south.

'What's the idea?' Adams asked curiously.

'I think we've overlooked something. It looks to me as though these Slitherers 'home' every night in one particular place, much the same as birds go to roost, and unless I guess wrong they have

chosen Coxwold. Don't you see the pos-
sibilities? If we can get them all bottled up
in one spot — all of the British ones, that
is — we can really work something out to
destroy them.'

'Why Coxwold?' Adams asked, thinking.

'I get the impression that that's where
they're roosting, if you can call it that.
Didn't you see thousands of them pass
over a while ago, heading south?'

'Can't say I did.'

'We'll see anyway. I don't think they
were aiming at London, so Coxwold is
the next reasonable possibility.'

Adams nodded but he did not say
anything more. He was, in truth, weighing
up the peculiarity of the situation — that
he and Norcross were speeding through
the mellow summer night to investigate
the rendezvous of devilish, thought-
absorbing flying reptiles. It was all so
alien, so utterly at variance with the
normal way of life. More than once in
the past few weeks Adams had wondered
if he were not perhaps dreaming the
whole thing.

It was close to midnight when they came eventually over the brow of the hill that led direct to the Coxwold road. Norcross put on the brakes and he and Adams sat looking at the distant darkness that represented the village itself. Neither of them spoke, and there was not a sound in the air. The soft night wind blew around the open car and overhead the stars were shining mistily.

'Gives you the heebie-jeebies,' Adams said finally. 'Don't know how you feel about it.'

Norcross nodded slowly; then he came to a decision. 'We'll walk the rest. The noise of the car engine might attract the attention of the things. Here — take one.'

He rummaged along the shelf under the dashboard and dug out two acid guns. Adams looked vaguely surprised.

'Two specimen guns from the Government for the Vigilantes,' Norcross explained. 'If anybody needs a couple it's us. They're filled with nitric acid. Be enough to protect ourselves anyway. Come on.'

They scrambled out of the car and began to walk along the lonely road that led down to Coxwold. The quietness was almost unnerving. It gave him the impression that they were being watched, but evidently this was not so for nothing stirred.

So, in due course, to Coxwold itself — for all the world like a ghost town. The houses were unlighted and deserted. No lamps were glowing in the main streets. There hung over it all an air of funereal gloom and uncertainty.

'This way,' Norcross murmured, and from experience he led the way directly to the great cornfield where the Slitherers had had their birth. He was fully expecting to find it a blackened waste from the acid onslaught, but not quite so black it proved to be.

A few yards from the entrance to the field, gained by means of an ancient gate, the two men stopped and looked. And looked again, in the uncertain starlight.

'That blackness isn't acid burn — it's Slitherers!' Norcross whispered at last. 'Thousands of them packed as closely as sardines in a tin.'

'And heaven help us if they attack,'

Adams muttered.

'That's something we've got to risk. In any case we don't need to go any further: I merely wanted to satisfy myself. So far as we can tell this birth-field is jammed tight with the brutes from side to side and end to end. Attack them at night when they're like this and the chances are that we'll eliminate the lot of them.'

'If they're all here,' Adams said. 'Somehow I can't credit that.'

'Why not? I don't pretend to understand the habits of the Slitherers, but it does seem obvious that they have some kind of homing sense that leads them to come here at night . . . We'll check back on it and find out how many of them are not here at night.'

Adams nodded and, as quickly as possible they began to retrace their way to the car. They had evidently not disturbed anything for there was no evidence of attack. Nonetheless they did not breathe freely again until they were well on the way back to London . . .

And the next day Norcross put his plans into action. From all points of

Britain he asked for reports to be sent of Slitherers activity at night, and since almost every town, village, and hamlet in the British Isles was covered he felt sure of fairly conclusive results. Hardly had he done so than he found Government representatives on his track, hard on the heels of the Burlinger massacre.

'Something drastic has got to be done, Mr. Norcross,' declared the head of the deputation — who arrived in the laboratory in mid-morning. 'I may say that my superiors are gravely disturbed at the lack of progress since you took over this Slitherers business. What has been done? Nothing! Nothing at all!'

'My team and I are scientists, not magicians,' Norcross replied calmly. 'If we were fighting something earthly we'd know what to do — but the Slitherers are alien, and that makes it enormously difficult. Progress *is* being made, though it may not be apparent immediately.'

'You know what happened at Burlinger last night?' the official snapped.

'Certainly I do, and I am sorry to — '

'Never mind being sorry! You should

have been alert enough to issue some kind of warning to the people of Burlinger. There is grave disquiet everywhere after that business, and I'm afraid the people won't stand for it much longer. Vigilantes and acid guns may be all very well, despite the expense, but they are not enough. We've got to have something concrete, Mr. Norcross.'

'Such as?' Norcross asked coldly.

'Is it not possible to forecast where these Slitherers will strike next, and so evacuate the town in question? Surely they have some kind of fixed habits from which inference can be drawn?'

'Certain fixed habits, yes — but a preview of where they will strike isn't one of them. If you are dissatisfied with the efforts my team and myself are making we can — '

'No, no,' the deputation leader hastily interrupted. 'Not *dissatisfied*, Mr. Norcross, but we certainly would like to see more results.'

'You probably will before long. I am on the verge now of trying a new line of attack. In the meantime, if the Slitherers attack anywhere else in force it will have to be combatted as best it can.'

Upon which the deputation retired, leaving Norcross in a bad temper. To himself, and to Adams, he raved about the crass ignorance of the Government and its lack of scientific understanding; then he resumed the now seemingly endless job of finding something to destroy the specimen Slitherer without destroying everything else at the same time. As on previous occasions a day's work drew a blank.

'Do you think water would kill these things?' one of the team questioned. 'It might, you know. There's been no rain for ages, and that may account for the fact that they're so thriving. And as far as I can make out from the reports there is no sign of them in ponds, rivers, or oceans.'

So water was tried, without result. Grim-faced, Norcross looked at the specimen Slitherer in its glass case and then turned to meet the scientists around him.

'I think,' he said, 'we should suspend our experiments until I get reports of the night activities of these creatures. It may well be that the matter will be lifted out of our hands and given to the air force if my idea is correct, and the Slitherers assemble in one particular place each night, we've as good as won the battle. All we have to do is attack them in force from the air while they are resting en masse. And that will be that.'

In theory, Norcross's idea was straightforward enough, but he had overlooked the fact that the creatures had something he had not reckoned with — absorbed intelligence, and that intelligence was of a very high order indeed for flying reptiles.

5

The chaos spreads

Next morning, in accordance with Norcross's request, reports began to pour in from every part of the country, and by noon he was jubilant. Nowhere, it appeared, was there any evidence of the Slitherers being active at night — at least insofar as Britain was concerned — but many observers had seen clouds of them moving south at high speed.

'This is all we want,' Norcross said, as Adams stood by his side. 'We'll pass the information on to the air force and see what happens.'

Wires began to hum. The air ministry was contacted. An attack on the Coxwold field was timed for exactly midnight that night. At the very least, Norcross was counting on the decimation of at least seventy-five percent of the things, and the remainder would be mopped up in due course. The weapons would be bombs, some explosive and others acid, with incendiaries wherever they were needed.

It was all arranged: everything was perfect and the night was calm and free of mist. Norcross remained at the laboratory, along with Adams and a few of the more interested scientists, kept constantly in touch with the situation by radio. At 11:45 p.m. hundreds of 'planes took off from various centres, all converging on the Coxwold field for midnight. People below, in bed and out of it, wondered vaguely what was going on as the droning from the heights impressed itself upon them and then slowly faded away.

At midnight exactly the 'planes converged — but, not a single 'plane had any chance to drop its load. From below, the packed thousands of Slitherers came rising up with stupendous speed, also apparently working to a plan. They smashed through observation windows and wiped out the crews before they had a chance to do anything. In the case of turbo-prop aircraft they deliberately entangled themselves with the propellers and jammed the motors. They clung to and snapped fuse-lage, tore off undercarriages, battered and slammed their way into turbo and jet air-craft alike. Like living razors they sheared through wings, smashed bodywork, and in less than fifteen minutes — despite the cost to themselves — they so demoralised the raiders that they had to turn back, many of them fighting inside the cabins with the thinking, reptilian hordes.

The news of the debacle reached Norcross in jerks over the radio, and the last report of the 'planes — what was left of them — crawling homewards, half of the crews dead and the 'planes themselves hardly holding up.

'It just can't *be*!' Adams said, astounded, as the radio went dead. 'What's *happened*? Reptiles even if they are alien, can't get the better of modern 'planes, surely?'

'Don't be a damn fool man. They've done it haven't they?'

Irritably, Norcross swung away from the radio, his brows drawn in thought. At last he slammed his hand savagely on the bench.

'I should have foreseen this, I suppose.

The creatures have an unusual intelligence, thanks to what they've absorbed from human beings and I suppose instinct — always strong in the lower orders — warned them of what was coming. So they attacked . . . '

He swung as the telephone jangled. Quickly he snatched up the instrument.

'Norcross speaking.'

It was the O.C. of the South London air detachment, and he did not sound particularly cordial, either.

'I suppose you've heard what's happened Mr. Norcross?'

'I've heard, yes. What's the exact picture?'

'Far as I know at present every 'plane has been damaged in some way or other, and we've lost about fifty percent of the men. It's no use making a second attempt. We'll have to think up something else — or rather you will. Thought I'd advise you that I'll have to report this debacle to the Government. They're waiting for the results of the attack. I'm afraid you'll have some pretty stiff questions to answer, Mr. Norcross.'

'I know — I know,' Norcross sighed. 'All right — and thanks for the information.'

He rang off and stood thinking. Then he realised that the rest of the scientists were looking at him expectantly.

'I expect from now on that I'll be out of a job,' Norcross said bitterly. 'The powers-that-be certainly won't take kindly to this lot.'

'Getting rid of you won't solve anything,' Adams said. 'We will probably hit on something eventually, no matter how many failures we have at first. Where's the guarantee that anybody else, having to start from scratch, will do any better?'

'High officialdom doesn't think that way,' Norcross answered.

As it happened, high officialdom might have been inclined to soft pedal the business had not the Slitherers themselves precipitated things. For that night they did not follow their usual procedure and spend the dark hours in rest: Instead they descended on London and attacked it in force.

So unexpected was the whole business and so savage its execution, it was over within an hour. Further, it was arranged that it happened simultaneously at different parts of the city, thereby throwing police, fire brigades, and ambulances into confusion. The lack of warning was the worst thing of all. The first intimation anybody had of the attack was a single Slitherer hurtling through a closed or open window and thence settling on its victim with leech-like tenacity.

Hundreds of men, women, and children were attacked — and died. In other cases it was entire families that were wiped out. Old, young, rich, poor — it made no difference to the merciless hordes. By the time they withdrew and fled south some two thousand people had perished in the city and the news was only just struggling through to Government headquarters and the media.

Norcross got the full blast of the information in his morning paper. By mid-morning, following a sleepless night, he had been summoned to an extraordinary Government meeting at Downing

Street, there to face the Prime Minister and the heads of the various services, together with representatives of other countries.

'You realise, Mr. Norcross,' the P.M. said gravely, 'that this business of the Slitherers is getting beyond all bounds, and that science — headed by yourself — has not contributed a single thing towards combatting the menace?'

Norcross's lips tightened. 'I am doing my *best* sir, and so are all those who work with me. We cannot do more than that — but if there is any scientist who can tackle the business more efficiently then I'll gladly make way for him. Frankly I doubt if there is such a person, because in this matter it isn't a case of how skilled a man is or how many degrees he has got. It is best in the hands of a man who has studied the business from the beginning, as I have. I've been engaged on this matter since the time of the giant cornfields.'

'Quite so, but nothing has been accomplished, and that is the point I have to consider with the public demanding action, more especially so after last night's attack on London. A thing like that happening every night, could very soon reduce the population to panic.'

'I'm perfectly aware of it, sir — but under the present conditions I can no more stop it than tell the sun to cease shining.'

'What exactly *is* the difficulty? Cannot the resources of modern science exterminate these pests? We seem to deal with most of the things that trouble us, from ants to house flies — yet we're at the mercy of *these*. Why? It doesn't make sense.'

'These things are from another world,' Norcross said quietly. 'There lies the answer, sir. The things we tackle on *this* world are exterminated easily because we have had experience of them for many years. Here we are faced with something new in structure — '

'But surely they can be killed, like anything else?'

'Yes — but only with difficulty. They have the power of reasoning — which is something no Earth creature of the lower order possesses. They can *anticipate*, and that is our problem. They have not this power when they are born, but they absorb it from every victim they attack. They suck brain knowledge as the Earthly leech sucks blood. Because of that they must have a very good knowledge by now of all Earthly methods, and the knowledge will increase as they make further attacks. They themselves will increase ten and thousand-fold by the simple process of dividing and sub-dividing. That is their biological method of sexual reproduction. We can never find each one individually and kill it, therefore we are trying to locate a point where they all congregate, then devise something to slay them as they sleep. We thought we had it when the air force attacked, but once again they anticipated.'

'I see.' It seemed that, to a certain extent, the light had dawned for the Prime Minister. 'And these Vigilantes which you have instituted? Are they of any use at all?'

'Only as defensive units. They contribute nothing to the destruction of the

Slitherers themselves. On the other hand, they can prevent attack, providing they are in a constant state of preparedness.'

The P.M. reflected for a moment, then, 'I tell you in all seriousness, Mr. Norcross, that these gentlemen and myself had arrived at the conclusion that it would be as well to depose you — but now I see what we are fighting I think it would not be a good policy to change horses in mid-stream. The struggle must go on . . . Er — I am no scientist, but have you tried electrocution?'

'Get the things fenced in — as we hoped they would be last night,' said the air chief, 'and then electrocute them by remote control. I cannot see that that should be beyond reason.'

'It's worth a try,' Norcross agreed. 'I'll do it. There is also another line of action which occurred to me a little while ago — find out what these creatures eat and poison their food. Unless, once again, instinct warns them of danger. Anyway, sir, we have many ways to try yet.'

'Very well,' the Prime Minister agreed. 'For the time being we will let it rest at that.' So, feeling he had escaped disaster by the skin of his teeth, Norcross returned to the laboratory, and to his colleagues gave an outline of what the Prime Minister had said.

'Electrocution?' Adams repeated. 'What on earth does he mean by that?'

'It's an idea anyway,' Norcross said. 'I think we might do worse than wire the Coxwold field from end to end and then stand by to switch on the juice by remote control when the Slitherers come home to roost. Electricity is something they won't have time to argue with or even think about.'

Norcross did not waste any time about the business. With those of the scientists who were expert electricians he went to work to have the Coxwold field prepared. It was a job that took all day, whilst Norcross himself, Adams, and one or two others kept constant watch of the skies for a sign of a returning Slitherer. Nothing happened, however, and towards four-thirty in the afternoon the job was done. The entire blackened area of the field was a fine mesh of criss-crossed wires, all joining finally to one main cable that, in turn, was linked to a high-tension power wire overhead. When the time came a plunger system could put 10,000 volts through the mesh and, it was hoped, Slitherers would go with it.

'There's no sense in going home and then coming back,' Norcross said, glancing towards the service truck that had brought them. 'We want to be on hand for when the Slitherers return. Better go as far as the next town and have tea, then return.'

This they did, and at five-thirty returned to a point on the dusty road where they could just see the field. Down at the side of the road, connected to the overhead pylon, was the plunger that would make the field live.

'I don't know about you,' Adams remarked, 'but I don't feel any too comfortable here. This truck's an open one. What happens if the Slitherers spot us as they return to the field?'

'We'll get out of sight under the truck. Somebody's got to be in the front line if we're going to get any action at all — and this time it's us.'

If any of the scientists felt like backing out they did not say so; so they watched the sky intently, smoked cigarettes, talked of cabbages and kings, and waited. And waited . . . The mellow sun sank lower as the evening took over, and at length the twilight was on the land. Conversation had ceased now. The sky was the sole focus of attention.

Then suddenly Adams pointed. 'Look!'

Norcross watched for a moment, a faint slowly growing cloud in the far distance. He sprang to immediate action.

'Here they come! Underneath, boys, and have your acid guns ready.'

For a second or two there was terrific activity as every man jumped down from the truck and scrambled underneath it. There, lying flat, they waited — tensed for anything that might happen.

'What's our next move?' asked the scientist who had appointed himself as the chief electrician. 'The plunger's over there, by that pylon.'

'We wait until they're all settled,' Norcross replied. 'We've got to have *all* of them to accomplish our purpose — then we act.'

Silence again. Dust blew into the men's faces as the wind stirred restlessly. There was also another sound — the swish of thousands of Slitherers as they cleaved the air and then presumably settled down on the carefully laid mesh. Time and time again the swishing sound came and, each time, the hidden men tensed for an attack which never came.

'I don't think we've any need to worry,' Norcross said at length. 'The Slitherers only attack what they can see. They don't seem to have any power of scent.'

They fell silent again, and at length as the twilight faded into darkness, the sound of returning Slitherers ceased. Only the soft night wind made any sound at all.

'Okay,' Norcross murmured. 'We'll risk it now. I'll come with you. I don't expect any man to do what I would not do myself.'

With that he wriggled gently from under the truck and slowly stood up; then for a second or two he stood surveying the almost incredible picture the Coxwold field presented. From end to end it was packed with Slitherers, lying on top of each other in some cases, but in any case so tightly jammed there was not an inch of room between them. There must have been thousands.

'Strange, the way they love that field,' the scientist commented, coming to Norcross's side. 'Rather than overlap into any of the adjoining fields they lie on top of each other. Darned if I can understand it.'

'Nor I,' Norcross shrugged. 'In fact I can only just see them in the afterlight. Get busy with that plunger. We'll never get more of them together than we have now.'

The scientist nodded and moved silently towards the pylon, beside which was the plunger. He glanced once over the terminals, up to the power wires themselves, and then drove the plunger home . . . Nothing happened. But then one hardly expected that anything would be visible. Presumably a destructive electric current had passed through the

Slitherers, and that was that. Yet somehow the two men had not expected such a tame result.

Vaguely puzzled the scientist came back to where Norcross was standing.

'Okay?' he asked.

'Yes — I suppose so,' Norcross answered uncertainly. 'I'd like to have seen something for our trouble. We'll wait a moment and see if anything happens, and then take a closer look.'

Motionless, they stood watching in the gloom — then, as the moments passed and there was no sign of movement amongst the assembled hordes, Norcross jerked his head.

'Come on. I think we can risk it.'

They ducked under the wire surrounding the field and advanced step by step towards the danger area. It certainly seemed as though they had been successful for there was still no sign of attack — then the scientist, a little in advance of Norcross, stopped suddenly and pointed.

'The main power wire,' he breathed. 'It's cut through!'

It was a second or two before Norcross

151

grasped the significance of what had been said. Certainly the main power wire that led back to the plunger had been severed. Which in turn meant that the Slitherers themselves must have done it! Somehow they had figured out that the wire meant danger for them . . . And that meant that not one of them had died.

'Back!' Norcross whispered, his voice strained. 'Back as fast as you can. These brutes are perhaps only waiting for us — '

He commenced to move, and that precipitated things. Suddenly, in a solid mass, perhaps a hundred of the flying horrors rose. Norcross saw them coming as he glanced back over his shoulder and he whipped out his acid gun, but the first concentration of attack was on the scientist, who was a little nearer to the main mass of Slitherers than was Norcross.

In one swooping dive the flying horrors descended and the scientist dropped to his knees as he aimed his acid gun. A few of the brutes instantly shied away from the jet of the gun, or else to the ground, wriggling as the acid ate remorselessly into them. But for those that fell more came, and still more.

Norcross let out one mighty yell for help — which carried to the men waiting around the service truck — then he plunged to help his hard-pressed colleague, only to realise within a few seconds that there was nothing he could do. Acid or otherwise, the reptilian brutes were everywhere, increasing rapidly in numbers, and in any case Norcross had all his work cut out to defend even himself.

He ducked, twisted, and lashed out, firing his acid gun at intervals, all the time struggling towards the wire fence at the edge of the field, and the truck beyond it — and throughout all the time he had a confused vision of his colleagues also fighting for their lives, and using their acid guns to good effect.

Norcross had the one advantage that he had been attacked once before, so he knew exactly how to ward off attack. Before any of the flying horrors could get a grip on his limbs or forehead he brushed them off and delivered a stab of acid. Or he caught hold of the reptiles and slammed them down on the iron-hard ground. He was, without doubt, the toughest of all the men the Slitherers had to beat.

And still they came, cloud after cloud after them, aroused now completely. Panting and blood-streaked, Norcross reached the fence and tumbled over it. He broke into a run and gained the truck, scrambling beneath it. Here, with a makeshift roof over his head, he felt a little safer — but even then the reptiles made every effort to dart under the truck, until the constant stabbings of acid proved too much for their ardour and the attacks slackened.

Norcross wiped his face and waited for his colleagues to follow his example. Maybe five minutes passed and then Adams came blundering into safety, smothered in dirt and his hair awry.

'Dodged them!' he panted. 'Dodged them by hell! First experience I've had of them at close quarters, and I don't want another.'

'Where's the rest of them?' Norcross questioned.

'Last I saw they were still fighting. Guess it's every man for himself.'

Adams breathed hard, flexed his finger round the the trigger of his acid-gun, and pointed into the gloom beyond the truck. Grey shapes were darting there. Some slithered around the under chassis of the truck, and then flashed out of sight, evidently sensing it meant death to risk going any further. But slowly the scene became quieter, and at last there was a calm. Only the restless night wind, and nothing more.

'The others,' Adams said, turning a shadowy face, 'are a long time coming back!'

'Why not face it?' Norcross asked bluntly, 'They're not going to come back — any of them. The Slitherers have got them.'

'But there were nearly half a dozen of them! Strong, intelligent men — '

'And for that reason they overestimated their own powers, and underestimated the Slitherers. They stayed to fight it out, which is crazy. It's no disgrace to retreat before these things, like we did. Nobody gives you a medal for turning into an imbecile a little while before you die.'

Adams was silent for a moment or two, and then he began to move.

'I'm going to see what's happened to them. I can't credit that they're dead.'

'They are — you can take it from me — and watch yourself!'

Adams nodded, and scrambled to the outside. Then he slowly stood up. Norcross watched his legs for a moment or two, then he also emerged and looked about him. Everything was quiet again and the Coxwold field was obliterated with a mass of grey shapes.

'Gone back to roost,' Adams said at last. 'If you call it that.'

Norcross nodded. His attention was upon six dim shapes in the near foreground before the Slitherer region itself. There was no denying what the shapes were. Norcross drew Adams' attention to them.

'There's your answer,' he said quietly.

Adams swung savagely. 'Well, they're not going to get away with it! Every one of them was a decent fellow. Every one

156

had a home and family responsibilities — and they're sacrificed to a lot of stinking, dirty reptiles from some other world. We'll see about that!'

He began to move urgently but Norcross gripped his arm.

'Wait a minute, man! Where are you going?'

'To repair the cable break! Once I've done that I'm going to ram home that plunger . . . Let go of my arm, can't you?'

'Not likely. I'm not going to let you commit suicide. You'll have to get within a few yards of the Slitherers to repair that cable break — and you're not going to do it. We're going back home.'

'But — '

'Shut up! Come on.'

Adams hesitated, then as Norcross still pulled on his arm he finally relaxed. Silent and grim-faced he climbed up into the truck and sat down next to the driving seat.

'This,' Norcross said, settling behind the wheel, 'is not going to be easy. When I start up the engine the things will probably awaken to a fresh attack. Here's my gun — use it along with your own if you have to. I'm going to drive like hell and trust to luck. Right?'

'Okay,' Adams grunted, staring at the distant field in the starlight.

Norcross started up the engine and the roar it made seemed shattering in the silence of the night. From that instance he did not even hesitate. First, second, and top gears followed each other as fast as he could make it and he drove off down the country road in a cloud of dust and blaze of headlights.

It was mainly the dust that acted as a smokescreen. Some of the Slitherers rose from their resting place and hurtled into the dark to give battle, but the job was too difficult for them. The dust blinded their efforts, the jetting acid was a powerful deterrent, and then again Norcross was driving at high speed. All things considered, the Slitherers finally thought better of it and called off the attack. Norcross began to breathe a little more freely as he struck the main London road.

'Up to now we seem to have achieved nothing but the deaths of half a dozen valuable men,' Adams said bitterly. 'What's next?'

'I don't know,' Norcross muttered. 'If the things would only behave like the reptiles they really are a lot of our difficulties would be solved. It's their damnable quality of being able to use human reasoning that defeats us every time. We'll have to report what's happened, of course — '

'Naturally. I still don't see why we can't use every damned 'plane the air force has got and simply rain an absolute hell down on that field. I know it's a case of the sledgehammer cracking the walnut, but at least it would achieve something.'

'If that sort of onslaught held out any promise I'd have done it long ago — but it doesn't. No matter how violent the attack some would be bound to escape, possibly blown aside by the explosion. Those few survivors would very soon reproduce themselves and we'd be no better off. Besides, we know what happened to the air force when we tried it last time. It would be the same this time.'

'But surely weight of numbers — '

'No,' Norcross said stubbornly. 'It wouldn't do.'

He remained silent after that, obviously turning things over in his mind. Meantime he still drove like the devil, landing the truck back in London towards two in the morning. He ran it into the big back yard of the Ministry building and then alighted.

'Neither of us is in shape to work out anything more tonight,' he said, as Adams alighted beside him. 'We'd best sleep on this and then tackle the problem afresh. I've got an idea in the back of my mind that requires some developing . . . '

'What sort of idea? Anything I can work on, too?'

'Not really, but you gave me the idea in the first place if that is any consolation to you.'

And further than that Norcross refused to be drawn . . .

★ ★ ★

At dawn, which meant something like half past four at this time of year, things began to happen. London was still sleeping, as were most of the major cities, so the Slitherers met with little opposition when they attacked. True, one or two Vigilante parties saw them coming and immediately started up the siren-warning system — but there was not time to make an organised defence against the things, particularly as they came in such driving hordes. Most certainly the tens of thousands of the things that descended on the city in the early hours could not have come from the Coxwold field alone. There must be other 'sleeping fields' somewhere to account for the numbers.

And this time it was not so much of an attack on the populace as carefully planned, methodical destruction. The guidance of intelligent, reasoning thoughts was obviously behind it all. The bewildered Vigilantes with their almost useless acid guns tried to fathom what the Slitherers were driving at, and finally it occurred to them that the crippling of transportation and communication was the objective aimed at.

One enormous army descended on the

main city power stations just as the night shift was coming to an end. Startled men, utterly unprepared, found themselves abruptly in the midst of cloying leeches that descended as thick as leaves in a winter gale. They came through the big open doorways in a never-ending stream, and only stopped when somebody had the wit to shut the doors . . . But the respite was only temporary and with a shattering of glass, the multitude continued through the windows. Mercilessly and methodically they exterminated every man in the building, sucking him dry of intelligence and leaving him a mindless idiot, dying on the steel gangway where he had been struck down.

When every man was wiped out the Slitherers moved to a new plan. Their scissor jaws snapped cables, sawed through vital wires, ripped down delicate wiring and instruments, and committed suicide in destroying the main electrical arteries through which power was surging. Hundreds died in jamming and clogging the generators; more thousands died in choking the immense water turbines.

Until power stopped and the absolute limit of chaos had been reached. Only then did the survivors — still in the thousands — retreat.

If this disaster had been limited to one powerhouse it would have been bad enough, but it occurred at all the five major powerhouses of the city. It was all over before police and fire brigades could do anything about it, and the hordes next descended on the telephone exchanges. Here indeed they had a field day. The multitudes of wires were all severed, the switch panels smashed from repeated bulldozer blows, and the staffs wiped out in the same fashion as the powerhouse crews. There was left behind a knee-deep ocean of dead Slitherers who had died from deliberately hurling themselves against objects in the frenzied determination to destroy themselves . . .

Only then, with the telephone exchanges and powerhouses at a standstill, did the remaining Slitherers withdraw, and even then there were thousands of them. North, south, east, and west they travelled, like queer migrating birds without wings, and

London gradually awoke, to the comprehension that something was not as it should be.

For one thing there was no electric light or power; there was no radio; and telephone calls produced no result. Plunged into chaos, as it had often been in the past, the city produced every available emergency squad to deal with the situation. The most crippling and savage attack yet by the remorseless products of another world had come — and gone.

And it was this situation that faced a harassed Norcross when he arrived at the Ministry laboratories towards nine o'clock. He could not telephone Government headquarters, so he went personally — and despite the early hour the nature of the crisis gave him audience with the Prime Minister.

'You don't have to tell me what has happened, sir,' he said quietly, as the P.M. looked at him grimly across his desk. 'The Slitherers have attacked in force.'

'The Slitherers,' the Prime Minister said, 'have acted with all the ingenuity and cunning of an invading army, Mr.

Norcross — and as such they represent the most terrible army we have ever had to face. Men and machines we can combat, and destroy — but these vile, brain-sucking reptiles are something different. I don't need to tell you that this is only the beginning of a vast campaign? At least I think so.'

'Vast campaign?' Norcross repeated, trying to think straight.

'This London onslaught was not localised. Five minutes ago a guided missile message reached me from the United States — the only possible way to send news with radio and submarine cable out of action. It will interest you to know that every one of the major American and Canadian cities have suffered similar onslaughts to ours and communications are completely disrupted. In many instances martial law has had to be proclaimed until the chaos can be sorted out. In every case Slitherers have been responsible . . . Now,' the P.M. continued, hunched forward, 'is it conceivable that these reptiles will leave the issue as it now stands?'

'Very unlikely,' Norcross admitted.

'They must have some liaison between each other to arrange these attacks as they have done . . . I imagine they'll attack again, and again.'

'Precisely. In any kind of struggle it is expedient to destroy the enemy communications first, and that is exactly what the Slitherers have done. They haven't troubled this time to attack the population, only the staffs connected with their objectives. Plainly the time has come, Mr. Norcross, when they are aiming at dominance. For a reason best known to themselves they are trying to oust human beings — and unless we do something very quickly they'll succeed! What is behind all this I don't know. Unless you do?'

'I believe, and I think I am right, that it is purely the beast mind trying to gain the upper hand, as the beast always will. I know these things are reptiles, but their minds work as the beast works. They would never have got this far but for their theft of human intelligence. As you say, they've got to be stopped quickly, otherwise, with their almost limitless powers of reproduction, they'll finally infest the Earth from beginning to end and human beings won't even have a look-in.'

'Precisely. When we last conferred, Mr. Norcross, I said I was not in favour of changing horses in mid-stream, and I am still of that frame of mind. You have had enough experience with the Slitherers to be the one who will finally discover a way to vanquish them — along with the scientists of other countries, that is. But you realise we must have action quickly?'

'Naturally. All I can promise is redoubled effort, and a new line of attack . . . ' Norcross hesitated. 'We tried your own suggestion of electrocution last night, with disastrous results, I'm afraid . . . ' and he went on to outline the circumstances.

'A great pity,' the P.M. sighed. 'Particularly as we have lost so many useful men. However, no blame attaches to you since in war there must always be casualties . . . What is your next proposition?'

'I'm trying something entirely new, based on observations I have made concerning the Slitherers. No direct action will be taken until I have determined if these various conclusions of mine are correct. Let me command the co-operation of all the best scientists and I dare to think that I may have the answer.'

'Very well,' the Prime Minister assented. 'And I say again — speed is essential.'

With that, a gravely thoughtful Norcross returned to the laboratories at the Ministry. The Ministry, as such, had almost ceased to function and the place had come into world-focus as the headquarters of those trying to combat the Slitherer menace. Norcross did not waste any time. He summoned to his side — as soon as possible owing to the disruption in communications — the best men of science he could find, to replace those who had been killed, and when they were all present he outlined his new theory. Urgency was given his efforts by the report that during the morning a second attack had been aimed at the centre of London, this time concerned with railways and road means of communication. The Slitherers were undoubtedly determined to clinch the crippling gain they had already achieved — and it was in the very shadow of the menace, never knowing but what at any moment they might be attacked and killed, that Norcross outlined his intentions.

'Firstly, gentlemen,' he said, 'I think our approach to this business up to now has been all wrong — and I'm as much to blame as anybody. We have tried the bull-at-a-gate method without the least success. We're never likely to have any whilst these things can think for themselves and anticipate us. There is the other way: the study of their behaviour and the breaking down of what, to them, has become accepted practise. Now first: what do these things feed on? Can any of you answer that?'

Apparently nobody could. The scientists just waited for Norcross to continue.

'I don't think they feed on any substance as we know it,' Norcross continued. 'We discovered some time ago that they propel themselves through the air by utilizing the magnetic lines of force. To do that they must be basically electrical, therefore it would seem from that that they do not so much need food to restore their energies as recharging. Like a battery . . . Logical?'

The scientists looked somewhat surprised but they nodded slowly just the same.

'Last night, Adams here let a chance remark slip.' Norcross glanced at him. 'It was this remark that set me on a new line of thought. He commented that it was surprising how much the Slitherers seemed to love the Coxwold field, so much so that they return to it every night and — note this — when on the field they even lie on top of one another rather than overflowing into the adjoining field and have more room. That raises a question in my mind: is there something unique about the Coxwold field which hasn't so far occurred to us?'

'In the matter of re-charging, you mean?' one of the scientists asked, thinking.

'Exactly!'

6

Radiation 250

'But what could there be?' Adams questioned, plainly surprised that his own remark had started wheels moving. 'The Coxwold field is the same as any other — except for the fact that after all the acid we tipped on it, it's a little more dead than anywhere else. I can't see any special significance, Norcross.'

'Then why,' Norcross insisted, 'do these Slitherers — most of the English ones anyhow — come to that field every night and stop there? We have assumed it was because the field happened to be their original birthplace, but I fancy there may be a deeper meaning.'

'Even so,' a biologist pointed out, 'there must be many such fields in England to accommodate all the tens of thousands of Slitherers which now exist — and they do exist as witness the latest attack on London.'

'There may be dozens of such fields, or areas,' Norcross agreed, 'all of them having something in common with the Coxwold field. We have to acknowledge that these things want sustenance. From our test Slitherer we know that no normal food does the trick, therefore it must be radiation. What is significant about the Coxwold field? I think it would pay us to find out — and quickly.'

'We could do it by day,' Adams said. 'The things seem to leave the place clear then.'

'Exactly. Now I do not pretend to be an expert on radiations, particularly when I don't know what I am looking for. Who among you gentlemen is fitted for a job like that?'

'I'm Travers,' one of the men said, raising his hand. 'I've had plenty of experience in solar radiation. I'm also employed at the Greenwich observatory on solar matters.'

'Right; I'll want you,' Norcross said. 'Who else?'

'I might be of use,' another man said. 'Marsden's the name. I've a lot to do with electrical matters, particularly in the physical laboratory.'

Norcross nodded. 'Good enough. That's all I need. You'll come along, Adams, as a matter of course. The rest of you gentlemen I shan't need to bother further for the moment. Thank you for your help, and when I need you again I'll call on you.'

His 'team' picked, Norcross was ready to go into action. He delayed only long enough to receive a series of reports — which showed the Slitherers were still at work in various parts of the city, and which also meant they were unlikely to be at the Coxwold field — and then he set off in a fast brake with Adams, Travers, and Marsden, and a considerable amount of technical equipment.

Throughout the journey they kept a constant lookout for the flying invaders, but no sign of them marred the limpid blue of the summer sky.

Norcross, at the wheel, pulled a sleeve over his brow.

'I've almost forgotten what rain and a cool wind are like,' he commented. 'It's no wonder these Slitherers are having a heyday. It must be a paradise for them.'

'Think wet weather, when it comes, will make any difference to them?' Travers asked, gazing out onto the dusty fields.

'Don't think so. Might lower the speed of reproduction, but that's all. And by that time, unless we do something, they might have won the day.'

The subject had taken a grim slant, so none of the men spoke on it further. They were content to think their own thoughts as the journey progressed, and at length, amidst clouds of dust, the brake swung into the lane that bordered the field they wanted. With a squeak the vehicle halted and for a moment Norcross sat looking at the unmoved, and unmoving, shapes in the field next to the vital area — then his eyes strayed to the wire still hanging from the power pylon as on the previous night.

'I suppose,' Travers remarked after a moment, 'those are last night's victims?'

'Correct. There wasn't time for burial — no time for anything except to get out.' Norcross shrugged fatalistically. 'After all, this is war, even if of an unusual nature.

There isn't time for the burials when under fire. We might do something about it right now, however. Seems quiet enough.'

He descended from the brake and surveyed the unbroken blue of the sky. Nowhere was there any sign of a Slitherer.

'Better bring the equipment along,' he said. 'We'll do the job as fast as possible in case of trouble.'

With four of them at work it did not take long to unload the various instruments; then they headed for the Slitherer field, by-passing the fallen bodies at a fair distance. These corpses, somehow, acted as a reminder of the urgency of their task.

'Now, here's the area.' Norcross said, as they stood on the edge of it. 'You can see how we wired it up. A regular wire mattress, in fact, but the devils broke the main feed cable. Now, what we have to discover is: is there anything peculiar being radiated from this particular field?'

Travers nodded and began to sort out his instruments. Marsden began an inspection of the ground, but shrugged his shoulders when he had finished.

'Nothing that I can see,' he said. 'Maybe Travers can make a better job of it.'

Travers' instruments, when set up, looked rather like a sextant in design, except that everything was dominated by a dial resembling a voltmeter. Norcross looked at it curiously. At the moment its big needle registered zero.

'If there's anything in this ground this detector will register it,' Travers said. 'We use it sometimes to register radiation of solar frequencies from the Earth. It's on the principle of the Geiger counter, only it doesn't click. Now, let's see.'

He switched it on and immediately the needle on the dial jumped to 250. Carefully he turned the nozzle of the detector itself, thereby gradually encompassing the entire field, and the same reading was maintained throughout. Though it was all Greek to Norcross he watched interestedly just the same.

'Any luck?' he inquired presently.

'Tell you in a moment. I haven't finished yet,'

Travers' experiments were apparently by no means at an end. He fitted a thin lead shield into place, which apparently shadowed the main detector chamber from the grilling overhead sun, and then he went to work again. The instrument needle still registered a steady 250 no matter which part of the field the instrument was carried to.

'What does it all mean?' Mardsden asked, and Norcross and Adams also waited eagerly for the answer.

'Notice this scale?' Travers asked, indicating it. 'As you can see it covers the entire field of solar radiation — ultra violet, infra red, and all the lot. Ultra violet, the highest of the lot, registers 198, yet here we have a needle swing to 250 which carries us far beyond the ultra violet field into other radiations, the X-rays, gamma rays, and cosmic waves, and beyond that. Deep into the higher range of the spectrum. Radiation even shorter than cosmic waves, which are supposed to be the limit.'

'You mean the radiation is solar?' Norcross asked. 'Given off by the sun?'

'It is given off by the sun, yes, and up to now has fallen into the category of unknown radiations — in other words, one of the many solar radiations given forth and unidentifiable. We've known of it for long enough, but haven't paid particular attention to it since it seems to have no useful purpose. Now, however, we face something else. With the detector masking the sun, by means of a shield which is known to be proof against any sort of radiation — at least for a short time — we still get a reading of 250 from the earth around here which proves the radiation is absorbed by the ground and then reflected again with all its original strength. Radiation 250, as we'll call it for convenience, is being reflected from the ground here with one hundred per cent efficiency. Let's see what the rest of the ground around here has to say and then I might be able to form some sort of conclusion.'

To complete his investigation did not take him long, and Norcross, Adams, and Marsden looked at one another as they saw the needle on the instrument sink to zero immediately the Slitherers' field was left behind.

'Very, very interesting,' Travers said. 'I think we're on to something, Norcross. Do I explain here, or shall we move to safety?'

'Explain here, and be damned to Slitherers,' Norcross answered promptly, with a brief glance at the empty sky.

'All right — here it is as near as I can get it. The Slitherers' field is loaded from end to end with some kind of material which reflects Radiation 250 with full effect. Towards the edges of the field the effect fades off and soon drops to zero. What it is that reflects 250, I don't pretend to know, and it may be at any depth down since the ground won't stop the radiation being received or given off. That it happens to be limited to the Slitherers' field is purely a coincidence. The inference from all this is that the Slitherers come to this field to absorb 250, and when they lie on top of each other the radiation is transmitted from one body to the other — as in the case of electricity.'

'There must be other fields or areas like this,' Norcross said, thinking. 'This field alone can't accommodate the numbers of Slitherers which now exist.'

'There can be other areas, just as easily as there are certain areas of Earth loaded with radioactivity only detectable by Geiger counters. There's nothing unusual about the situation. The Slitherers have proved to us that certain spots of Earth are sensitive to absorbing and transmitting solar radiation 250. In itself it is harmless enough — to human beings anyway. But to the Slitherers it is life blood, the recharging energy by which they keep alive.'

'So far, so good,' Norcross reflected. 'But it doesn't entirely answer the problem. 250 is given off by the sun, you say. In that case the Slitherers wouldn't be any worse off if we destroyed this field — or rather somehow prevented it from giving off 250. They would absorb it from the sun. Even cloudy weather would not stop it since the radiation must obviously come through the clouds.'

Travers narrowed his eyes thoughtfully.

'Assuming we could neutralise this field, we would cut down the stimulus to the Slitherers by fifty per cent. One thing seems obvious: they must be stimulated day and night, hence their return to a place where they can get 250 once the sun goes down.'

'At times,' Adams said, 'they have attacked at night.'

'Perhaps when they have felt more revitalized than usual,' Norcross answered. 'It isn't their regular habit to strike at night . . . And there is another thing. Why should the sun going down affect them? Won't it pour its radiation 250 right through the Earth?'

'Not very efficiently — if at all. In passing through the Earth itself the radiation, in common with all the other short wave ones, will encounter barriers of lead, nickle iron, and dozens of other strata, all of which will weaken and dissipate the efficiency. No; I think we can discount that. The issue as it stands means that the Slitherers live by solar radiation in the daytime, and live by the emanation from the ground at night. I fancy that with that stimulus cut by half they might run into trouble.'

'That test Slitherer of ours evidently keeps going by whatever radiation it gets from the sun in daylight hours,' Norcross mused. 'Naturally, the laboratory building and the glass walls of its case will not block the radiation ... Good! We've learned what keeps the damned things alive. There are two things now to do — Find out by aerial survey how many more 'recharging' fields there are, and also see, from our test Slitherer, how much it is reduced in efficiency if 250 is cut off altogether. From that we can calculate what a fifty per cent cut would mean.'

'Fair enough,' Travers agreed, starting to dismantle his instruments. 'And returning to more mundane matters hadn't we better do something about these bodies?'

'And also,' Marsden put in, 'remove this electrical mesh from the field? Henceforth we don't want to give the Slitherers any warning of what we're driving at. It seems to me, that if they weigh things up from the human angle, they will think we've admitted defeat if we remove all signs of the electrical attempt.'

'Okay,' Norcross assented, and whilst Travers completed the packing up of his instruments the carefully laid electric mesh of the previous day was gradually dismantled and removed. The line to the power wire overhead was also dealt with by the experienced Marsden, and the plunger taken away. In any case, even had they hoped to attempt further electrocution ideas it would have been no use with all power cut off — at least temporarily.

'In regard to these bodies,' Norcross said, surveying them, 'we'd better call the ambulance — Damn, there's no 'phone!' he broke off in irritation. 'All right, we'll tell the ambulance men in the first town we come to, to move the bodies to the south London mortuary. Then there can be a decent burial for them.'

'Only thing,' Adams agreed; then he gave a little shiver. 'For God's sake, let's get away from this spot and have some lunch. It's giving me the jitters.'

* ＊ ＊

If the public expected any respite from Slitherer attack following the early morning onslaughts on powerhouses and telephone exchanges, they were sadly mistaken. Even while Norcross and his helpers were heading towards Coxwold there descended on London fresh hordes of the flying reptiles and this time they concentrated their attention chiefly on railway stations.

The chaos they produced was appalling. The stations themselves were reduced to disorder. Staffs and intending travellers were likewise attacked, which meant fleets of ambulances to add to the general confusion. Engine drivers, mates, and plate layers also came in for annihilation, and the points of the railway lines themselves were jammed with dead Slitherers who had deliberately committed suicide in their determination to jam the junctions.

Worst of all were the signal box controllers. In both the normal and electronic signal boxes a sudden splintering of the windows gave warning of what was happening, and a few seconds later men were fighting with everything they had got to ward off the relentless hordes. They failed, as had so many before them.

Not only the railways suffered but also long distance freight wagon crews. In this case no more than half a dozen Slitherers attacked, but that was sufficient to so distract the driver and his mate that wagon after wagon met with disaster, overturning, colliding, and — in the case of inflammable fuel transports — exploding entirely.

Nearer home in the city centre the ordinary bus traffic suffered. In the clogged bottle necks of the city streets the hurtling reptiles had a field day, smashing against bus windows and shattering them, killing passengers and crews, causing endless confusion, collisions, and hold ups.

Nobody was safe anymore, and most people realised it. All day long, in the blazing summer sunshine, the Slitherers kept arriving in inexhaustible numbers to continue their battle against hapless civilians. Vigilantes fought back with their acid guns, and whatever weapons they could find, but there seemed no end to the attackers and no limit to the fury of their onslaught.

Whilst the main fury of the attack was concentrated against lines of communication, isolated Slitherers did a good deal of damage also. They came and went in offices and factories, always leaving their trademark of death and imbecility. The isolated Slitherers were everywhere, and totally unexpected. They attacked without rhyme or reason. The humble little typist or the pot-bellied executive, the royal personage or the crossing sweeper — all went down before the lithe, twisting, grey fury of the horrors.

Even the men who toiled desperately to get the telephone exchanges and power-houses going again were not immune, though they were surrounded by Vigilantes which, to some extent kept the fatalities down. By noon telephone communications should have been restored, until it was discovered that the Slitherers had methodically severed all telephone wires leading out of the city.

So it continued into the afternoon. The city was thick with the flying hordes. They squirmed on buildings, monuments, trees, pylons, and window ledges. They flogged buses, harried and destroyed human beings, smashed shop windows, and wrecked all semblance of order in transport. In one whole day of onslaught the city was reduced to a complete chaos. Nobody knew what anybody else was doing, and it was impossible to use telephones and send for help. Disorder was complete.

On the fringe of the city proper, in the Ministry of Agriculture building, Norcross and his fellow scientists worked on. They knew of the happenings around them, chiefly through word of mouth, but there was nothing they could do about it. In any case their energies were better devoted to the task of discovering the solution that was within their grasp.

At the moment the attention of the four men was devoted to the test Slitherer. There, Norcross insisted, lay their first experiment. Around the Slitherer's glass case on three sides — those facing the sunlight drenching through the window

— were heavy lead screens borrowed hastily from the Physical laboratory. According to Travers the screens were thick enough to block the 250 solar radiation. The fourth side, away from the sun, was left clear for viewing purposes. Right now the quartet stood watching the Slitherer as it moved at intervals about its case.

'Sure it doesn't matter about leaving the fourth side open?' Norcross asked presently.

'Quite sure. The radiations travel as straight as rays of light. Block the three sides facing the source and that's all that is necessary.'

'We'd better be right,' Norcross muttered. 'From the way things are going in London we shan't have much more time for experiments. The things will beat us to it . . .'

'Wonder if it's the same everywhere?' Adams asked. 'I mean overseas? If other countries are suffering the same kind of onslaught.'

'Probably they are . . . It would seem that the Slitherers have suddenly decided on direct and violent action, and I see no reason why they should limit themselves to Britain . . . '

For a while there was silence. Some fifteen minutes without any noticeable change in the action of the encased Slitherer.

'This thing hasn't been fed, I suppose?' Travers asked, watching it.

Norcross shook his head. 'We tried every darned thing — liquids and solids, but it refused the lot. Which seems to confirm that its food is electrical.'

'Mmmm, looks that way. Wish we could get a reaction.'

But no reaction came during the afternoon and, much dejected, the four retired to the canteen for tea and sandwiches. During the process of eating them they got wind for the first time of the magnitude of the disaster that had struck — and was still striking — the city. The news came by way of single emergency sheets of newspaper, printed on manually-operated presses.

LONDON BELEAGUERED

189

Such was the headline, and the remainder of the sheet — on both sides — was given over to the details. Norcross scanned through them and then handed the sheet to Adams.

'I'm going back to the lab,' he said. 'I want to be knowing whether we've got a fighting chance to win this war, or not.'

Adams and Marsden went with him. Travers followed more leisurely, reading the newssheet as he went. When he came upon Norcross, Adams, and Marsden again, in the laboratory, he found them standing still staring at the Slitherer case. And the important thing was that the grey reptile was motionless on the case's base.

'Is it possible?' Norcross breathed. 'Or is it just resting?'

He moved forward slowly and rapped sharply on the side of the glass case. Usually this had the effect of stirring the Slitherer to instant and violent life — but not this time. It did not move in the least.

'I think we've done it!' Norcross said, his eyes bright, as the three other men grouped round him.

'Give it a prod,' Adams suggested.

Norcross hesitated. Opening the top of the case to do as Adams suggested meant risking a lot of things if the reptile were only shamming or partially unconscious.

'Go on — risk it,' Marsden urged. 'This thing isn't as intelligent as its contemporaries because it's done no brain-sucking. We've got to take the risk if it awakes we'll deal with it somehow.'

Norcross abandoned all caution and reached for a long stainless steel testing rod. Then he opened the case a fraction and fished the rod inside until he was prodding the Slitherer steadily . . . Nothing happened. It was like poking the hard outside of a motor tyre.

'Pull it out,' Adams said. 'We can't tell any other way, and we're ready for trouble.'

Norcross nodded tautly, completely removed the top of the case, and then reached inside with the long-handled tongs. He noticed as he lifted the Slitherer out that it remained rigid as a board, which seemed a promising sign. In a few moments the thing he hoped for was confirmed. The thing's eyes were glazed over and rigor mortis had already set in.

'Well, you were right, Travers,' he said, with a thankful sigh. 'Cutting off 250 brings death in approximately two hours.'

'Which demands a little calculation,' Travers said. 'This thing only had 250 to rely on during the daylight hours, and none at all at night. Which means it must have been able to tide over the night hours with what it had stored up during the day. The point is: can the other Slitherers do the same?'

At that Norcross felt his heart sinking again. He glanced up, looking harassed.

'If they can we're no better off. We won't do any more than just make them tired. In winter of course the sun won't be above the horizon for as long as it is now — Damnit, we'd never survive that long anyhow.'

After a moment Adams said: 'Isn't there another point we should take into consideration? The majority of the Slitherers are very intelligent due to their attacks on human beings. It is a well known fact that the higher the intelligence is the more

192

physical energy there is consumed. On test, a hard working mathematician consumes more energy and needs more stimulus than a trench-digging labourer. On that premise maybe the Slitherers would succumb much more quickly from a nightly loss of 250 than this one, which was never of the intelligent variety.'

Norcross's eyes had brightened again. He looked at the other scientists questioningly.

'It's a good theory,' Travers said presently. 'Even if we don't kill them we may at least weaken them enough to get the upper hand.'

'All right then, what do we do?' Norcross asked. 'How do we neutralise the Coxwold field, and others like it?'

'There,' Travers reflected, 'is our problem. We have to do two things — a: stop the sunlight and radiation reaching the field, and b: stop the emanations being given off by the field. Even cutting off the sun's radiations from the field won't stop the field itself from emanating for a long time to come. We must block both, but the point is how?'

'Cover the field with lead,' Norcross suggested. 'That will block the 250 from being given off by the field, and it will also stop the sun from handing it out. 250 won't go through lead, surely?'

'It will in time,' Travers sighed. 'Remember that 250 is even shorter in wavelength than cosmic waves. The neutralisation would only be temporary, and again there is the possibility that in their frantic desire to get stimulus the Slitherers would gnaw through the lead. It's a soft metal and they'd easily destroy it. Most certainly they would if their lives depended on it.'

There was silence for a moment, then Travers seemed to come to a conclusion.

'I think the matter is best referred to Greenwich observatory. I'll get in touch with my superiors, who know far more about 250 than I do, and see what they have to suggest. Meantime, Mr. Norcross, why not get the air force to work — tonight if possible — and pinpoint the exact areas where the Slitherers rejuvenate themselves? That will take most of the night if all England is to be covered.

194

In the meantime I'll find out all I can.'

'Fair enough,' Norcross agreed, glancing at his watch. 'And I'll have to contact the air ministry personally with no 'phones in action. Adams — Marsden, you'd better come with me. If the air force can send out three squadrons of investigating planes one of us will have to go with each squadron otherwise the pilots won't know what they are looking for.'

Travers headed for the door. 'And I've got a tidy journey to make through a city that's anything but normal. See you when I have some news — even if it gets to tomorrow.'

★　★　★

Throughout the late afternoon and through the evening the Slitherers continued their depredations on London, completely disorganising whatever attempts were made to rectify matters. Towards mid-evening, missile reports, sent across the Atlantic, were received, reporting much the same conditions on the other side of the water.

The Slitherers were definitely working to some kind of plan, keeping in touch with each other by some form of telepathy, which distance evidently did not weaken. And, as far as could be seen, their sole object was the removal of the human race from the scheme of things.

Meantime both Travers and Norcross were busy — particularly Norcross. Once he reached the Air Ministry he did not have much trouble in securing that which he needed. The Prime Minister had already swept possible obstacles aside with the result that Norcross's request for three airplane squadrons, completely equipped with still and movie cameras, and protected by a ring of fighter planes who would deal with any Slitherers who happened to interfere, was promptly agreed to, and the time was set for midnight for departure from the London base.

It was arranged that Adams should go with one squadron, and Marsden with another, while Norcross of course would go with the main force. From London the planes would travel south — the exact

196

area to be covered in the first night being worked out on the map — and afterwards, on succeeding nights, the midland and northern areas of the country would be covered. Scotland and Wales would use their own air forces, once word was got to them telling them what to do.

The only trouble Norcross foresaw was the possibility that the Slitherers would continue their onslaughts into the night — in which case they would not return to the 'rejuvenating' bases. And if this happened it would throw the whole theory into doubt, also. However, he need not have worried for promptly at sundown the hordes began to retreat, and within half an hour London was left clear to sort itself out after the day-long battle. When he heard the news at the Air Ministry, brought by motorcycle dispatch rider from Government headquarters, Norcross felt a little better. It seemed to prove anyway that there was definite need for the Slitherers to restore themselves in energy. For the moment that was all that mattered.

And, at midnight, the 'planes set off

and swept into the misty dark of the summer night. Under Norcross's directions, his own particular squadron headed for the Coxwold field and, sure enough, it revealed itself as crammed from end to end with the creatures. Immediately flares were dropped, bringing the scene into scintillating brilliance, and the still and movie cameras went into action.

It was all over in a few minutes and, undisturbed by Slitherers, the 'planes went on their way on a toothcomb search. It was by no means an easy job with most of the countryside below heavily misted — but searchlights and flares succeeded in penetrating most of the barriers and, wherever a rejuvenating area was detected, it was immediately logged, photographed, and pinpointed.

As the night wore on and the 'planes droned back and forth, Norcross admitted to himself a definite surprise at finding so many of the rejuvenating grounds. Evidently the Slitherers had a natural instinct for finding them. Certainly it was something close to a shock to locate nearly twenty of the grounds in the course of a night, and upon return to base the other two squadrons had a total of thirty six, and thirty three. Which, of course, immediately explained where such vast hordes of the flying reptiles kept coming from. And there were still the Midland, Northern, Scottish, and Welsh areas to be investigated.

Once he had returned to London base, Norcross went home — dog weary after his hours of activity in the grilling heat. But the next morning, early, he was back again at the Ministry laboratories — and so again were the Slitherers back on the attack on London, carefully destroying all the repair work that had been accomplished by desperately working men and women during the night.

Travers turned up not ten minutes after Norcross, and there was a gleam in his eye that foretold of success.

'Any luck?' he asked Norcross.

'Good enough. We located dozens of the grounds, and they're all carefully marked on the area maps, together with photographs . . . I've no need to go on any further investigations, and neither have the others. The air force knows now what to look for . . . But how did you get on?'

'The Greenwich staff, and myself, spent what was left of last evening until sundown, and every bit of this morning after sunup, making tests of the 250 radiation, or rather making experiments to prevent its operation. Ultimately we landed on this.'

Travers took from his pocket a small box. Inside was a package of tissue-paper. He unwrapped it and brought to light an oblong slide of deep purple glass, so purple it seemed almost black.

'What is it?' Norcross asked curiously. 'One-way glass?'

'Yes, but with a difference. It's used a good deal in solar observation when visual observation has to replace photographic study. Have a look through it.'

Norcross held it to his eye. Everything seemed perfectly clear and yet somehow the light had gone out of things. It looked like the most perfect anti-dazzle shield ever devised.

'So?' Norcross asked, interested.

'You can look at the photosphere of

the sun through that — for hours if need be — and there'll be no harm done. It's semi-polarized glass, made to a special formula. It sifts out infra-red, ultra-violet — and cosmic and 250 radiation. Permanently and completely. It turns them aside, even as it turns light waves. That's why there is no dazzle. In a modified form it is the same type of glass that is used for the goggles of ultra violet lamps. Proof, too, against X-rays, of course. Technical name is hexomalene glass. But it is essential it face the right way. Placed the wrong way round it lets everything through. The right way is to have this peculiarly ribbed surface — see it like hair-thin draught-board pattern? — facing the sun. Then if you're behind it you're quite safe.'

'And that's our answer?' Norcross asked, surprised at the simplicity of it.

Travers did not answer immediately. Putting the glass oblong on the bench he picked up a big hammer and brought it down on the glass with all his strength. Nothing happened. There was not even a crack.

'That is the complete answer,' Travers said. 'The enormous strength of the stuff. No Slitherer ever born will be able to break it or chew through it. Only drawback is the cost when manufacturing a lot of it, but as the price of safety I reckon it's worth it.'

'What do you propose doing with it?' Norcross asked. 'Covering over all the field areas?'

'There's a better way.' Travers put the slide in his pocket. 'Let us try for a moment to put ourselves in the place of the Slitherers. Assuming we found our energy sadly impaired through being unable to absorb the stuff at night. What would we do?'

'Rest,' Norcross suggested, logically enough.

'And where to do that? A hundred to one the Slitherers will choose the same place as at night. That means they'll come back to the rejuvenating grounds — which of course won't do them any good because the earth-source of 250 is cut off.'

'But they'll have the solar source,' Norcross pointed out.

'Not if that too is masked. They can get the solar source in the ordinary way anywhere during the daylight hours, but my hunch is that they will return to rest, thinking they can revive themselves that way, for I'm not giving them credit for being able to reason out that 250 is the sole reason for them being alive . . . So then, assuming they return to the resting grounds, we'll have them both ways. The more they stay at the resting grounds the weaker they'll get.'

Norcross nodded slowly. 'You've got something. A ground sheet of this glass, and then some kind of roof as well to cut off both ways?'

'I'd suggest a dome with a single entrance and a sliding door fitted for release by remote control. Don't you realise that when all these Slitherers are resting we can trap them wholesale? Whole fields of them. We've got them both ways. We reduce their energy to zero, and if we can we'll trap them as well. In about a day and a night a dome full of the horrors will have passed out. Then shovel them away to the incinerators and leave the door open for any more beauties that may decide to take a rest.'

Norcross started heading for the door. 'I'm going to hand this information to the Prime Minister,' he said. 'I'll get him to sweep everything aside so that every possible factory is manufacturing hex-omalene glass. Tell Adams and Marsden your story when they turn up. Shan't be long.'

7

Domes of death

There was no hesitation on the part of the Prime Minister, and because he had supreme authority all the factories in the country capable of turning out hexomalene glass were immediately commandeered. With this in hand it only remained for Norcross and his colleagues to draw the designs of the 'domes' required, almost every one different because of the varying sizes of the fields concerned.

Men and women worked night and day from then onwards, and every hexomalene factory was guarded constantly at ground level and on the roof. It proved needless, however, for evidently the Slitherers were not aware that something was being manufactured for their doom. They continued instead their depredations on the principal cities, evidently rooted in the idea that if they could once cripple the main arteries of civilised life they could also gain a permanent upper hand and gradually, through rapid increase in numbers, wipe out human life altogether.

The air force, meanwhile, was hard at work plotting the exact positions where the domes would be placed, as well as operating a regular patrol to guard the transit of the domes from the factories to the required sites. At the actual sites work could only be done in the daytime as far as erecting was concerned: once sundown came the human workers made themselves scarce and gave the Slitherers a clear field.

One of the first and most urgent jobs of the radio engineers was the restoration of radio communications, quickly followed by the return of power and telephones. On every possible occasion they were harried by the Slitherers, but by this time humanity had arisen to appreciate the danger and the flying horrors did not find it so easy as of yore to wreck everything on right, left, and centre . . . The army in particular was fully mobilized and went to work to protect vital necessities. In consequence all essential services had their own army and air force protection and to penetrate it was more than the Slitherers could manage.

But the actual destruction of the horrors, en masse, depended on Norcross and his colleagues. Though air force and army could prevent attacks, they could not hope to break the ever-increasing swarms, so they just did their jobs and hoped for the best.

Sensing they could not break the wall of resistance that had been flung up against them, the Slitherers seemed to hit back by enormous increase in their numbers. There were reports of them from all over the world, except the coldest climes, and everywhere it was the same story of their steady, persistent onslaught against the foundations of civilisation.

Naturally, the hexomalene glass situation was passed to other governments and they too began an effective mobilization for manufacture of the stuff, at the same time marshalling their air and ground forces for protective uses, as well as finding the sites where the horrors rejuvenated themselves. In those latter days of the Slitherers the Earth's population resembled an overturned anthill, so immense was the activity in various directions.

Norcross's particular pet was of course the Coxwold field. Once he and his colleagues had figured out the dimensions of each dome for each field there was nothing more they could do, beyond supervision, and explaining to other dome supervisors exactly what was required.

The dome on the Coxwold field was one of the first to be erected, as rapidly as possible in the daylight hours. Matters now had developed into a race between multiplying Slitherers and dome erection, for the flying horrors were increasing at a phenomenal rate in every country — and even the break in the weather which finally came, producing high winds and rain, did nothing to slow down the fecundity.

Norcross's engineers laboured without ceasing during daylight. They were drenched, wind-blown, became involved in accidents, were often dog-tired, but still they carried on, always with Norcross right on the job — whilst Travers, Marsden, and Adams were acting as head supervisors in other parts of the country.

First came the flooring area, an apparently unjointed circle of deep blue glass, which took an entire day to manoeuver into place with powerful cranes. Once this was done the erection of the dome walls, by sections — each section being flawlessly fused into its neighbour by heat process — commenced. On the first day just the floor area was laid, but Norcross remained behind with a few of the engineers to watch how the Slitherers, returning from their day's depredations, accepted their new 'ground sheet'.

It was not possible to see much. For one thing the nights were much darker than they had been due to the rain clouds, and for another the distance was considerable in the interests of safety. Nevertheless, through powerful night-glasses, Norcross could make out that the hordes seemed uneasy on their new bed.

They were not as motionless as usual and betrayed a constant restiveness. Still, none of them left the area, which was a good thing. Evidently it had not dawned on their limited intelligence that they were being deprived of essential rejuvenating energy.

Norcross was particularly interested in the reports the following day reporting on Slitherers activity, but his heart sank a little as no decrease in fury or numbers was indicated. Travers, who also read the report before departing for his supervision duty, gave a shrug.

'Don't worry too much yet,' he said. 'We can't expect the effect to show instantly, and besides there are thousands of these devils which weren't on the Coxwold field during the night anyway. See at the end of a week how things are.'

So Norcross could do nothing more than hope for the best. He went to the Coxwold field as usual and supervised the erection of the walls and roof of the dome. Altogether, the job took two weeks — time in which there had been no report of lessened activity on behalf of the

Slitherers. Norcross was secretly worried for by this time dozens of fields throughout the country were overlaid with the glass and he had hoped for some sign of diminishment in Slitherer energy. Evidently the brutes were still getting enough in the daytime to keep them going. Unless they were drawing on reserve strength, which, sooner or later, would fail completely.

The completed Coxwold dome — the first of the thousands to be finished — duly had its sliding door ready to drop into place. It occupied about a quarter of one wall and was drawn up over the curved roof, held there by a spring catch operated by an electrical circuit. From almost any distance the catch could be released at a touch of the switch and so make the dome unbreakable and entirely enclosed. This indeed was to be the real test — the possible trapping of the horrors as they came to rest.

Norcross and his gathered men were more excited than they had ever been so far as, a mile distant and using night glasses, they waited to spring the trap.

The night too aided visibility in that there was a mellow autumnal full moon.

True to type, the Slitherers came in their hordes immediately after sundown, but for quite a while they flew around the completed dome with a certain suggestion of panic. Certainly they had seen the thing on previous nights and settled within the shadows of its half-completed walls — but now they had only one place by which to enter and maybe their mysterious intuitive powers gave them warning of trouble to come.

More hordes came, and still more. Norcross, silent among the engineers and equipment, waited with ever growing anxiety for something to happen.

'If the brutes shy at it we're going to be in a spot,' he commented. 'All that work — to say nothing of the other domes — for nothing.'

'Hardly for nothing, Mr. Norcross,' one of the engineers commented. 'They've got to settle somehow, otherwise they won't get any rejuvenation. That's the way they'll look at it.'

Norcross grunted something and lifted

the night-glasses. They did not do him much good. All he could discern was the wild scrambling and slithering of the creatures over the outer surface of the dome. There were so many of the creatures it was hard to tell there was a dome at all.

'I hope Travers was right,' Norcross muttered at length, lowering the glasses.

'About what?'

'About hexomalene being indestructible. The way these brutes are stuck on it they look as if they're destroying it.'

'Impossible,' the engineer said flatly. 'The stuff will hardly crack even under a pneumatic drill.'

Even though he had his doubts Norcross said no more — and he decided that he had evidently guessed wrong for, after a while, the Slitherers began to thin out somewhat and, little by little, they began to disappear inside the dome.

'What did I tell you?' the engineer murmured, after a survey through the glasses. 'Everything's going to plan, Mr. Norcross. You say the word when we spring the trap.'

'Uh-huh.' Norcross was tensely watching. He began to smile to himself as gradually the dome and sky cleared of the creatures and they gradually vanished from view — inside the trap.

'Okay,' he said at length, lowering the glasses. 'Spring it!'

The engineer nodded and promptly depressed the electrical switch.

'Good,' Norcross murmured. 'That's sealed them in . . . Nothing more we can do now so we'd better come back in the morning and see what has happened.'

★   ★   ★

In daylight it was only too obvious what had happened. Norcross and his crew discovered the dome entirely empty of Slitherers and the trap door still high up on the roof. From the look of things it had never been lowered . . . Indeed it had not. An examination proved that the lock itself, set in a metal frame, had been chewed to pieces, and though the wire leading to it was mainly imbedded deep in the glass, it had still been severed

214

where a small section of it left the glass to make contact with the lock.

So even yet the problem was not done with. It demanded another week of work to devise a lock operated by radio, with no outside wires. And the lock itself was set in a hexomalene framework and covered in at all points. Surely there was no chance of the Slitherers getting at *this*?

None, as event proved. That night, for the first time, Norcross and his engineers had the satisfaction of seeing the trap close at last on the slithering hordes, and the first really mighty blow for freedom was thereby struck. The information was immediately transmitted to the Government, and all other dome sites were advised to use the radio-type lock that was proof against the reptiles.

Morning brought a revelation indeed. The trapdoor was permitted to slide up under radio control and then, for a while, Norcross and his men stood waiting. They half expected trouble because they could not believe that they had got the upper hand of the situation. But they had, as their later investigation proved.

When, after half an hour, there was no sign of activity round the opened dome, Norcross led his little party forward slowly across the slushy field. He kept his acid gun at the ready and did not allow his attention to be diverted for a single moment. Thuswise he finally reached the dome and looked uselessly through the one-way glass into the apparently black interior. Then he advanced to the open section and cautiously peered round the edge of it.

'Great God!' he whispered. 'It's unbelievable!'

The others did not say anything even though they agreed with him. The huge area under the dome was jammed half way up the walls with Slitherers — to a depth of nearly three feet. They lay on top of each other and piled up against the inside of the dome in every available spot. And every one of them was dead. Already the fetid stench of decay came wafting out into the morning sun.

'Batch number one,' Norcross said curtly, recovering himself and putting his gun away. 'There's yet another reason for the rapidity of death, besides the cutting off of vital life radiation, and that's the fact that when the shutter is down the place is airtight. These things, there being so many of them, must have suffocated as well . . . All the better.'

It did not take long to contact London and order the necessary disposal squads to work, then Norcross checked up on the other dome fields and found that there was success there too. Suffocation and absence of 250 had brought death to tens of thousands of the hideous reptiles during the night, but even so the fight was not over until every one of the horde was exterminated . . . And this took many weeks.

Every night, following days on which the Slitherers' attacks by day noticeably declined, the watchers were there, ready to plunge down the shutters when every available Slitherer had settled to roost for the night, until at last, in the very early spring there came reports that no Slitherers had attacked, and none had returned to roost. There could only be one answer to that . . . they had all gone.

'Just the same,' Norcross said to his colleagues when they discussed the matter at the Ministry, 'I think it might be as well to leave the domes for the time being. There might be one or two still at large who have perhaps found a breeding ground in some distant spot, a means of utilizing 250 that has not been discovered by watchful humanity. And from one could spring two, and from two four and so forth.'

Many were the speculations of Norcross and the scientists in the quiet months that followed the victory. Some of the brutes might even be hibernating somewhere. After all, nobody knew anything about them or how long their hibernation periods were, even if they hibernated at *all*.

Yet still nothing happened and the grass grew around the edges of the blue domes. Because the domes belonged to the Government nobody did anything about them. They still stood even after Norcross was dead and buried and the advent of the Slitherers had faded in the memory . . .

★ ★ ★

The sun was pretty low in the sky when mine host had finished his story. I had been listening attentively and it came almost as a shock when he stopped.

'Like another drink, sir?' he asked, rising.

'After that I certainly would.'

'I'll be getting it for you . . . '

He brought me a beer, and one for himself. Sitting down again he looked speculatively towards the blue dome in the distance.

'An' that's 'ow it was, sir,' he said, shrugging. 'Norcross got the better of the whole thing, more by luck than judgment. The Slitherers vanished and only the blue dome showed that they had ever been here at all.'

'And all this happened something like sixty years ago?' I asked. And as he looked at me oddly I added, 'I'm taking a hasty guess at your age if you'll forgive me. You said it all happened when you were a lad.'

'Aye, when I was a lad. However, shortly after Norcross died — he was in the mid sixties when that happened — somebody started a scare by saying that a Slitherer had been seen in Central America. Later somebody else saw another one — And then another. Just isolated instances, as you might say but these folks seemed pretty sure. Scientists said it was possible some of the things had escaped to the impenetrable jungles of Central America and there found plenty of sunshine and 250 radiation from the ground, and had multiplied and survived the fate of their fellows.'

I gave a little shiver, and it was not altogether because there was a chill in the evening air either.

'How long ago was this?' I asked, and the farmer closed an eye speculatively.

'Not long. About ten years mebby.'

'Not a very happy thought to think that Slitherers might still be in existence!'

'No. That was why they left the blue domes, in case they might be needed again.' The farmer took a deep drink. 'I don't ever think they will be, myself.'

'No? Why's that?'

'Doesn't it occur to you,' the farmer

said slowly, his rustic manner of speaking suddenly vanishing, 'that many things might have happened to those few Slitherers which were given the chance to really evolve? The advance guard — the killers and plunderers — were the rudimentary form of life given birth by the accidental catalyst of the dextrone. Imagine if they had had the chance to evolve and multiply in peace! What they might have become!'

'Become?' I repeated rather stupidly, trying to understand why the farmer's manner of speech had changed so completely.

'They had the power to reason, and think,' he went on. 'True, it was stolen in the first place but it was hereditary. When a thinking Slitherer divided itself into two, the second creature also had that power transmitted to it . . . Imagine the picture then! Intelligent Slitherers evolving without interruption, and in the course of evolution one automatically moves away from the killing stage to one of reason, even as do humans in their evolution from the caveman to the high-thinking scientist.'

'Just what do you mean?' I asked deliberately, and at that he rose and looked at me. There was a look in his eyes that I could not fathom. An other-worldly look, somehow.

'Those few surviving Slitherers could — and did — increase their numbers indefinitely. They were a new form of life born without a native planet. The only planet they had was the one on which they found themselves. Owning that planet and strutting proudly about upon it were human beings, creatures who, in time, became lower in intellect than the Slitherers . . . Despite their now high intelligence the Slitherers in their reptilian form knew that slaughter would await them if they ventured into the outer world. What then should they do?'

I got to my feet and stood waiting. The other-world eyes were upon me.

'All they could do was use their powers of intellectual drainage — if I might call it that — on whatever human beings they happened to encounter and then, having the empty shell so to speak, transfer their mentalities into it and withdraw from their own useless and very repulsive bodies. Simply fill with intellectual frequency the brain cells which they had drained, and abandon their own bodies. You would call it death, but to a creature who lives by dividing itself death is death of the *mind*, not of the body. A Slitherer can, and does, abandon its body at will, so high is the evolution pinnacle now reached.'

I caught the beer glass with my elbow and it clattered down onto the tiled path. It did not break.

'Don't be disturbed,' the farmer smiled. 'The Slitherers have grown up now. Once they have a human body they can take another human body and marry. There can be children, half Slitherer-half human, or all Slitherer basically, depending on whether the two who are married have their own bodies, or have just — er — borrowed them . . . ' The farmer, if he was a farmer, looked toward the sunset.

'These things can't be helped,' he said. 'It just happens — some accident of life or creation. In this case because a girl dropped turkey paste sandwiches. I assure you the Slitherers mean no harm and not often do their intelligences go wrong. Of course, we have the maniacs, the criminals, the half-wits, and that they have increased in the past years doesn't really mean that the Slitherers are responsible . . . '

'I must be going,' I said abruptly. 'It's later than I thought. Thank you for the beer and sandwiches, and the most interesting story . . . '

I turned and hurried away from the inn as fast as I could go. Once I looked back towards the blue dome and wondered if the farmer had been spinning me a yarn. Then I recalled how he had reverted to highly intelligent conversation . . . Because of that I write this story, to warn you.

The man you play golf with, the girl who sits next to you in the bus, the man who brings you your milk . . . Any of them might belong to the new race that has come to Earth through no choice of its own. Any of them might be . . . a Slitherer.

CLIMATE INCORPORATED
THE FIVE MATCHBOXES
EXCEPT FOR ONE THING
BLACK MARIA, M.A.
ONE STEP TOO FAR
THE THIRTY-FIRST OF JUNE
THE FROZEN LIMIT
ONE REMAINED SEATED
THE MURDERED SCHOOLGIRL
SECRET OF THE RING
OTHER EYES WATCHING
I SPY . . .
FOOL'S PARADISE
DON'T TOUCH ME
THE FOURTH DOOR
THE SPIKED BOY